# THE WRITERS' CIRCLE
## AND OTHER STORIES

Also by Michael Gessner

ARTIFICIAL LIFE

BEAST BOOK

THE CUSTODIAN'S JOURNAL

EARTHLY BODIES

GLASS

LETTERS

ON LOCATION, ESSAYS OF PLACE

SELECTED POEMS

TRANSVERSALES

SURFACES

# THE WRITERS' CIRCLE
## AND OTHER STORIES

MICHAEL GESSNER

BLAZEVOX[BOOKS]
*Buffalo, New York*

The Writers' Circle and Other Stories
by Michael Gessner
Copyright © 2016

Published by BlazeVOX [books]

Printed in the United States of America

Interior design, cover art and typesetting by Geoffrey Gatza

First Edition
ISBN: 978-1-60964-238-9
Library of Congress Control Number: 2015957343

BlazeVOX [books]
131 Euclid Ave
Kenmore, NY 14217

Editor@blazevox.org

*publisher of weird little books*

# BlazeVOX [ books ]

blazevox.org

21 20 19 18 17 16 15 14 13 12 01 02 03 04 05 06 07 08 09 10

BlazeVOX

*Autobiography begins with a sense of being alone. It is an orphan form.*

—John Berger

*We are all orphans. Human communities, at heart, are orphanages.*

—Everett Extron

# CONTENTS

# THE WRITERS' CIRCLE
## AND OTHER STORIES

# THE WRITERS' CIRCLE

NO ONE UNDERSTANDS books like I do. That sounds ridiculous, I know, but it's true.

Our library has an annual book sale. Most of the books are the ones the library doesn't want anymore. The library director, who is also my supervisor, calls it deaccession. There's a word. The books are deaccessed, which means we get rid of them. When they become too worn, or too old, or under-circulated, that's when things start to happen. Some librarians call it weeding. We weed the garden, so to speak. Standard is two years, sometimes three, but if they aren't circulating, they're off the shelves.

We stack them on tables in the community room and try to sell them at our yearly book sale. If they don't sell we give them to Good Will. A few patrons donate books for the sale. This helps the library make extra income, but Ms. Wills intervenes and sells most of them on eBay or Amazon, so they never make it to the sale, but people come anyway, thinking they will find some treasure.

The Friends of the Library should oversee this, but they don't. Every month they meet for a luncheon. It's more of a social club, and they let Ms. Wills do whatever she wants. She takes care of their tab. They're pensioners and they appreciate this.

Popular novels, mysteries, regional histories get snatched up fast. People seem to like regional histories. They keep coming back for them. I think they like to read about where they live.

If Good Will doesn't sell the books, they try to get the senior center to take them. If the senior center doesn't take them, then they're thrown away. I've driven by and seen books piled up in the dumpster behind the Good Will outlet down on Main, destined for the landfill, but I rescue as many as I can.

Once I went to a book sale in another county. Ms. Wills sent me because she wanted to know about how other sales are managed. It was The State Valley Nurses' Association Annual Book Sale, and it was their inaugural event. I found a first edition of *The Grapes of Wrath*. It was like new—except for the pocket card—and it had a dust jacket that was just perfect. It was stamped inside. It said:

## D I S C A R D

The following year, I drove up for the sale again, and this time the nurses had an area cordoned off. Someone must have tipped them off that people were finding books that were rare or valuable mixed in with the thousands of other books they were given for the sale. There was a sign near the cordoned off area. It read: RARE BOOKS.

I strolled around and looked at one book, then another. Every book I picked up had a turquoise ink stamp that said: THE STATE VALLEY NURSES' BOOK SALE. The nurse in charge of the rare book section liked the new stamp. She said it was "distinctive."

If we had rare books in our library, we wouldn't stamp them like that. And we don't use pocket cards anymore either. The patron just gets a receipt with the book which says when it's due. We slip it under the flyleaf.

Stamps disfigure a book. It's like getting a tattoo that no one wanted. Something that says "I own you." Books are for everyone; they're meant to be shared. And if those nurses are trying to raise money and if they knew anything about books, they wouldn't be marking them up. Most collectors won't bother with a book if it has something that makes it look bad, like underlining, or doodles, or turquoise stamps. I want to tell the organizers of the nurses' sale about it although I don't think they'd listen to me.

All my books are special, even though they're usually beaten up by the time I get them. They're special because no one wants them. My books are sorted by what they are: history, biography, fiction, philosophy, and so on.

When my house started to fill up, and I was beginning to feel cramped, I went to the next logical choice, my garage.

Myron made shelves for me. He understands my book interest. He teaches communications at Dumphrey Community College.

One afternoon he drove by my house and saw me unloading books and offered to help. He saw they were stacked up in the garage, and he suggested shelves. Then, whenever he had time, he'd come over and put them up. Soon as a shelf was installed, it would get filled up. This went along o.k. until Eva, my sister, had an intervention. There's another word, *intervention*.

Poetry goes on the top shelf. Myron's a poet.

Sometimes I go out to the garage to read. Miss Itsy follows behind. We'll stay there for hours. There's a recliner I bought at a used furniture sale, and I curl up and read in it.

I'll be reading about ancient Egypt, or the Orient in one of those folio-sized art books, the kind you can just drift into the image and float around and become part of the picture. Other times, I'll read the essays of Montaigne, or Nin, or the stories of Proust, or Colette. Hours pass over me like clouds over the moon, and it's only when Ms. Itsy purrs that I am brought back to now. She brushes against my ankle and I know it's time to go.

Every so often my sister stops by. She lives across town with her daughter, Roxanne, but she wants to be called Roxy. She's 11. A tomboy. Eva drops her off if she has to work late which happens a lot because my sister is a tax account and works for a legal firm.

Mama left her the house because she has Roxy. I don't have a Roxy, but I told Eva I should be able to store some books down in her cellar.

She could do that much at least. Eva thought about it for a minute then said "No," she didn't want anything in the cellar. I insist it's my house as much as it is hers; it's where we both grew up, but she doesn't hear me. She doesn't have to remind me; she has the title. Her husband walked off and left her with his truck and Roxy. It's a half-ton flatbed. Roxy likes the ride. You can haul just about anything in it. Good for camping gear. Roxy's always trying to get me to take her, but Eva objects.

Was it Whitman? I can't recall right now, but I think it was. He said the book is more person than book. He also said the verses and the body are one. A book holds thoughts and feelings. It has a body, a spine, and a name. Each page is the flesh of a tree. I love the way they look and feel and smell.

There's a website for book smellers. I didn't know that until Ms. Wills pointed it out one day to me. I was examining an old volume of folk tales when she passed by and noticed me sniffing the pages. She said I shouldn't be doing that. "Pages are for reading," and suggested that I should talk to someone. If I didn't like that idea, then I could join a book smellers' site, which I didn't.

When books are donated to our annual sale from patrons, or local organizations, I can usually tell something about them from the scent they carry with them. It's like their history. The Nepal Shoppe in town sends over a few books each year, and they stock gift items, incense, figurines, and the books always smell like foreign spices. When I am assigned to deaccess, sometimes I might find a book I know will be discarded, so I'll hide it away.

That's how I found my commemorative edition of Longfellow. It's leather bound, but it's torn, and has the odor of ground hazelnut. It's next to the Bobby Burns book which is quilted, so the cover is puffy, and it's embossed with two maple leaves. Once they were red, but now they're faded. Its spine is broken, and it has the smell of aged leather and stale coffee.

Books from a smoker's home are distinct: cigarettes give the pages the odor of the way syrup tastes on tin, pipe tobacco offers the spices of fall leaves, and cigars leave a bitter smell. When cigars are burning, the aroma is pleasant—at least to me—but once the smoke has settled down in clothes or drapes, or books, it becomes acrid, as if it's resentful because it could not float away. Be free.

If a book has lived long in a house with Spanish cedar ceiling, it will carry the aroma of affection, compared to say, a book that has been in a home where cooking oil was used, then it's just harsh. My mother could smell lightning before a storm. She said it smelled like ozone.

People carry around with them all kinds of sensations. When anxious, they exude the distinct odor of cumin. Viciousness is steel. Some men simply manufacture this as if it's an endless supply and don't even know it. Zeal smells like flint. Chastity is starch. The aroma of wet loam is meekness. Humility; saffron.

Most smells don't have names. That doesn't mean we don't know what they are. If I'm waiting in a doctor's office, or in line at the market, I can tell about a person's emotional state, especially if they're near me. Although some smells are confusing, usually a dominant strain wins out. A stranger may send out the odor of fear, and the next minute it may change to excitement, and in another, relaxation which has the faint suggestion of milk.

Once I found a two-volume set on the art of Michelangelo with gilt-stamping and fore-edging. It's maroon cloth with lithographic images. Each picture of a painting or sculpture is protected from damage by a bound-in tissue guard. It's like onion skin. What's unique about this set is a hand-written note laid in by one of the previous owners:

> Voyager,
> May you find solace in the presence
> of the sublime among the heavenly forms
> reproduced in this book, surely a museum
> without walls. Let them accompany you

as loyal companions on your journey.

It isn't signed. The writing has flourishes, so maybe the writer was inspired, maybe a woman, maybe older. The paper is linen, possibly handmade.

At first, I thought it was nineteenth century, like the set itself, but the reference to the "museum without walls" is straight out of André Malraux who's not nineteenth century.

Malraux was all about imagination. He lived during a time of art replication, and art could be seen in private homes and collections, and you didn't have to go to other places like MoMA or the Louvre. I think his museum without walls was a forecast of modern technology and the internet. With the abundance of electronic images available today, when anyone can visit the great art museums in their own homes, that's just a global revolution that would have astounded him. It's beyond anything he could have expected. But mainly, Malraux's museum is about the human imagination not having boundaries. My garage is a museum without walls.

WE MEET ONCE a month to talk about how the library serves its' mission; how it can help those whom it serves. In our case, it's the village community. The entire staff is required to attend. It's better that way. At least Ms. Wills says so, because everyone feels like a member of a team. This is how we came up with the Writers' Circle, but it didn't start out that way.

We sit around a table. There's Ms. Wills, then Mr. Bynes, a facilities technician, though everyone knows he does janitorial work most of the time. He did fix the air condition once but that's only because someone forgot to plug it in. Then there's another librarian, an older woman who reads to the younger children, and her part-time assistant, and then there's me, Frances Stryk. I don't have an assistant. It's better that way. My sister calls me Fran. When our grandfather came to America, customs had a problem pronouncing his name, so they just wrote down something. They shortened it. They could have put in a couple of vowels. It would have helped. People always mispronounce it. It's 'strek.' Eva tells me if anyone asks, I should tell them it rhymes with 'wreck.'

We begin to brainstorm about how to serve our patrons. Mr. Bynes offers to paint the walls of the 'teen and children's section. These are two open rooms separated by a glass partition. He thinks the kids will like bright colors. It's like seeing their energy on the walls. One wall could be painted fuchsia, another orange, and another, ochre. Of course, it'd clash, but maybe it would be exciting for the children. Maybe they wouldn't think the library is a dull place. It would be more like them.

Everyone nods in agreement. Ms. Wills writes it down in her notepad.

The new assistant wants to exhibit materials of a local interest so people will come in to look at things like old hand bills used for elections, movie posters, newspapers of historical interest, like when the copper mine opened and the prosperity that followed, or the famous strike that didn't last very long, or magazines that featured our area as a tourist site, even though we don't have any tourists anymore, and the mine closed down years ago.

Ms. Wills considers the idea, but doesn't write it down, so we all know it's doomed. Then Ms. Wills has an idea of her own.

"I know what let's do, let's get a reading group together."

The older librarian shifts in her chair and looks at the ceiling. Someone clears her throat. No one's enthused because everyone remembers the last one.

One of us would be responsible for it. It was going to be me. I could sense it coming.

Ms. Wills went on about how a book discussion group was an important function of the library and brought people together in the pursuit of great ideas. Then she said, "How about you, Frances?"

Of course.

Before the meeting ends, the staff is asked to contribute to the local literacy campaign. It looks good when the library contributes. Shows people we care. I always give a check.

MY FIRST THOUGHT was to talk about the book people, how in Ray Bradbury's story, a future totalitarian government is committed to burning all the books and destroying critical thought and imagination, and the book people must live in isolation from the rest of society in their own community in the woods. Each person becomes a living repository of a single book by memorizing it, so the person becomes the book, and these are our heroes and wouldn't it be something if each of us found a book we loved so much we would commit our lives to it? That we would breathe it in, become it until it was us? I was all set to talk about this when we met, but I never got to it. I couldn't.

We advertised for about six weeks. We put posters up in the super market, at the bowling alley, and the community center. We even ran notices in the newspaper, *The Dumphrey Democrat and Chronicle*, plus some public service announcements on local radio. Myron made a point of persuading students to participate and promised them extra credit if they attended.

One afternoon, Ms. Wills came over to my desk to tell me she was ordering copies of a book for the group to read.

"Shouldn't the group make that decision?" I asked.

"How would they know? What if they all decided to read the latest blood-and-gore-ultra-libertine *du jour*? Or a confidential insider tell-all on abortion clinics, or personal narratives on euthanasia? What then? As a publically-funded institution, that would create attention, and eventually concern, and the very likely possibility of controversy. Let's avoid that, shall we?"

Ms. Wills wanted to stay with the "tried-and-true," as she put it, something from the 100 best books recommended by librarians. She instantly chose *Winesburg, Ohio*.

She thought it wouldn't be too demanding for them. They could read it in sections.

"Besides," she reasoned, "*Winesburg* contains stories and characters not far from their own lives, if you think about it."

I was thinking about it.

Ms. Wills had ordered the book already.

She ordered 35 copies.

If that wasn't enough, she could order more. This would save them from trying to buy their own copies which never seemed to work out in the past. There are always some people who can't afford to buy the book, or get distracted by their lives which go every which way and never get to it. I know people whose lives consist of nothing but detours.

Right after she went back to her office, my sister called. It's tax season and she'd been working late with a client, and would I mind looking after Roxy.

It was closing time, and I shut down my computer and arranged my desk. As I was leaving, I noticed Mr. Bynes over in the children's section. He hadn't lost any time painting the walls. He stepped back with his hands on his hips, scrutinizing his project. Everyone likes Mr. Bynes. He's very considerate, and has aqueous blue eyes. They're the most aqueous eyes I've ever seen.

ROXY WAS SITTING on the stoop when I arrived home. She had an overnight bag with her even though Eva didn't mention Roxy would be spending the night.

She gave me a quick hug, and soon as I opened the door, she scrambled by me and ran upstairs to my closet to get her jeans. I keep a pair for her on the top shelf behind some blankets. The mitts are there too.

I had some casserole left over, and while it was heating for dinner, we went to the backyard and played pitch. I bought Roxy a fielder's glove for her birthday, but Eva doesn't know. It's our secret. We played until it was dark. After dinner we watched horror movies. Roxy loves them.

After she went to sleep in the guest room, the 'phone rang. It was Myron with some good news. *The New Republic* had taken one of his poems, and he was elated. It was like getting a trophy. The poem is from a manuscript he's been shopping around, his little collection, *Chances*. It would be his first chapbook and the publication of the new poem will help him get it published, "if it ever does."

"It will happen," I told him. "It will. It just takes time."

He wants to celebrate. Maybe we could go out later in the week—dinner, maybe a drink.


THE FIRST NIGHT we had seven. There was an elderly couple, and a girl from the unwed 'teen mothers program at the high school. The twins, who were in eighth grade, left soon as they realized this wasn't a reading class, that is, they expected to be taught how to read.

"Better now than later," the old farmer said. He's Mr. Nestor, and he just started reading a couple of years ago even though he's in his 80s. It was after his wife died. Mr. Nestor said his favorite fictional character is Wild Bill Hickok. Wants to read more about him.

"What about it?" he asked.

The other members were still introducing themselves, but you could tell they weren't enthusiastic about Mr. Nestor's choice.

I've known people as old as 98 learn to read and write. They go to care centers and are encouraged by staff members, and once they know the basics they are forever grateful. It's amazing how many people don't know how to read or write. Most dropped out of school to help their families get by, which is almost a given in this county.

Then there's Everett who is so well read he could intimidate the others. He has a nose ring and tattoos and keeps to himself. He'll talk, but it's hard to get him to elaborate much. He probably needs time to get at ease with the group; everyone's a stranger to each other, at least for right now. His favorite hero is The Hulk.

He mentioned The Hulk soon as Mr. Nestor asked if anyone wanted to read more about Wild Bill Hickok.

Jo-Jo—from the unwed mothers' program over at the high school—jumped in and said her favorite character was Madame Bovary.

I wanted to bring everyone back to our goal. "It's wonderful you are all reading—something—and that you found characters you admire. That's a good start."

Next came the part where I had to explain that the book, the one we're all supposed to read, had already been purchased.

They were piled in stacks on the table. All 35 copies. I held one up.

"This book has everything in it," I lied.

"We should each pick our own book," Everett spoke up.

Jo-Jo concurred.

Then the others in the group nodded.

"Yes, perhaps. If we each chose a book, then each of us would be reading something different, something the others wouldn't know about because they wouldn't be reading the books other people are reading."

Plus I was thinking about what I was supposed to do with the books Ms. Wills purchased. We couldn't just ignore them, not now, after they were paid for.

They agreed to each take a copy and return after reading the first section. The first section is about a writer who had written about the people he knew in his town, "the grotesques."

After everyone left, the couple, who must be retired, stayed back a moment to reassure me they thought the book selected for the group would be "just fine."

The next day, when I was walking by Ms. Wills' office, she called me in to ask how things had gone with the group.

I didn't know what to say to her. I knew she knew. She knew very well. Someone told her, or she inquired. It's just her suspicious nature. She probably thinks if she knows everything that's going on it will help her keep a hand on things. But it didn't go well, and she knew it even before she asked me.

I said they were excited about the book choice.

"Really?" she turned her head a bit and looked at me and smiled like maybe she wasn't sure.

I began clicking my glasses. Whenever I find myself in a tough situation, I remove my glasses, hold the frame and tap the end of the plastic temple against my teeth. It didn't help matters any. Ms. Wills doesn't like me clicking my glasses, but I didn't stop, not because I wanted to annoy her, it's just a reflex, something that helps me when I have to figure out what to do.

"Did you have a good turn out?" she wanted to know.

This was another trick question. She knew exactly how many showed up.

"Just enough to make it interesting," I said.

Now, five is not the best number for a book discussion club, especially if some don't complete their readings. Anyway, I smiled my polite smile and walked off before she had a chance to say anything.

I thought that did it. I wouldn't have to face her again, but later in the day, she called me in. I expected an interrogation, but that didn't happen.

"We've been working together for quite a few years," Ms. Wills began, "and we know each other fairly well, don't we? Certainly we share a professional *rapport*. Don't you think it's time you called me by my first name? You can call me Blanche."

She pronounced her name like it was French, Blaonsch.

"I suppose I could," I said, knowing it would be difficult to get used to.

"Well, I'd like you to think about it. By the way, I wonder if you would be interested in a regional library conference that's coming up. I thought you might like to go. You would be representing the library, and you would be representing me, of course. It's in Philadelphia."

I almost choked. Would I? I was so excited I agreed at once.

It never occurred to me to ask why she wasn't going, or that I'd be leaving my books, or that I would be expected to present a paper. The paper is supposed to be on digitizing out-of-print journals. I've done research for Ms. Wills' presentations in the past, so the research part isn't anything new, but I hadn't presented a paper myself in a long time.

My graduate work was done in Philadelphia, and in the 10 years I've been at Dumphrey Library, I've gone to the city maybe three times. I don't know why. It's only two and a half hours' drive.

When I was a student, I loved to hike along the Wissahickon. It's where Poe took his wife Virginia for picnics when he lived in Philadelphia. I always knew about Poe the way you learn about authors from school anthologies, but I really got to know him through Mr. Graham. Even though I've never met Mr. Graham personally, I consider him a mutual acquaintance.

THE SECOND SESSION whizzed past me like a curveball.

Only two members—Jo-Jo and Everett—read what they were

supposed to have read. The couple claimed they had been too busy to complete the reading—a windstorm took off part of their roof—but they wanted to come anyway as a show of support, plus they wanted to get out of the house.

Jo-Jo complained that *Winesburg* wasn't something she could relate to, after all.

"Also," she wanted to add, "it made me uncomfortable."

Everett agreed. "Dated," he said. The book was dated.

I asked them what they wanted to read about.

Mr. Nestor wanted to read westerns. "Because they're real."

Everett was interested in new action heroes—transformers meet holograms.

The couple preferred domestic sagas with generations of families.

Jo-Jo was beginning a series, "Ladies in Literature."

Each thought everyone else should read what they wanted to read.

No one could agree.

That's when I had a flash of good luck.

"It's encouraging to see you all have such specific interests. And I'd like you to hold those thoughts until we meet again next week. I've invited a guest, someone I know you will enjoy and I think we can all agree on a book once we've heard our guest speaker."

They seem interested in that idea.

I hadn't invited anyone. My plan was to ask Myron to talk to the group about their reading selection problem. My hope was that he could find some common ground for mutual interest.

I brought up the idea to Myron when we went out later that week to celebrate the acceptance of his poem by *The New Republic*. The college administration had taken note, and asked him to give an interview for the student newspaper. He was supposed to answer questions like: why do you write poetry? When did you start? What are your other interests? Do you get outside? Do you like sports? And so on. The students get the questions to Myron before the interview. The administration likes this. They like it even better if they have the chance to read Myron's answers. But Myron's too busy for that.

We went to a new place, Italian. They have large portions, so we shared a lasagna dish and we each had a glass of red wine. When we were nearly done, I popped the question: would he mind talking to our book group at the library? It would mean so much ...

"Certainly," he smiled. "Don't give it a second thought."

That was a relief. He'd get them on track all right. I was confident of that.

When the bill came, I insisted on paying, after all, it was Myron's night. He earned it with all his hard work. But he refused, so we compromised, and split the check.

Later, outside in the parking lot, still elated over his publication, our hands slipped into each other's. It was almost magical, a natural fit, but it was only for a moment, then we both suddenly became self-conscious.

Soon as I got home, I settled in and began work on the research necessary for the conference paper. No sooner had I started, someone was at the door. It was Eva.

When I opened the door, I could see Roxy in the truck in the driveway. She waved 'Hi' but there was something strange; she had what looked like a bow on her head, then I realized it was in the shape of a butterfly. It was pink and sparkly.

Eva had dropped by on her way home from "Basics of Preteen Pageantry" at the 'Y.'

It was the first class. I didn't know she enrolled Roxy, and never thought of Eva as a pageant mom.

"They teach them *everything*," she said, "etiquette, poise, and social manners. Everything a child like Roxanne needs." She seemed spellbound.

"Does Roxanne like it?" I asked.

"Of course. What girl wouldn't?"

I didn't know what to say, so I told her the truth: that she caught me at a time when I was working on my paper for the librarians' conference in Philadelphia. The draft is due in a month.

Eva wanted to check in on me, which was kind of her. "That's the only reason I stopped," she said.

She was holding onto the door knob, and scanned what she could see of the house, which was basically my living room, and I knew she was doing this to make a point. Ms. Itsy was staring at her.

"It would make your life easier if you ordered your environment. Don't you think?"

She meant the books.

Eva pulled the door back, and made a sweeping gesture. "How can all of this be *healthy*?" She lowered her voice, "Really, Fran, isn't *one* library enough?" she said about where I work, and gave me a little sarcastic smile. "Honestly, in a year or two, I doubt if there will be enough room to walk through your place, you have it so cluttered up."

Eva then looked down at the cat. Ms. Itsy stared right back and purred her gravelly purr which isn't the best kind.

Eva brushed my cheek with a little kiss, and a tight smile, went down the steps to the truck, and backed out of the driveway with Roxy waving good-bye to me.

My sister has been voicing her concern lately, probably more than ever before. She's overextended with her work and all, not to mention Roxy. I don't tell her this mainly because she's my older sister, but she's too involved with too many things and she gets much too serious. Everything seems to be stressful for her.

But looking back on it, I suppose I should have agreed with her, maybe even straightened up the place, or promised to. Had I done that, maybe things would have been easier, but I didn't, and now I have to live with what happened.

Eva doesn't want me living alone. Not normal, she tells me. But once, when Roxy asked if Aunt Franny could live with them, Eva never answered her. I've never asked to move in, so it's a standoff. What I'm left thinking is this: she doesn't want me to live by myself, but she doesn't want me moving in with her either, even though the house is a two-story with lots of room. It's all right, and I'm all right too, with the way things are.

When she left, I tried to go back to my research, but I couldn't concentrate. I kept thinking of Roxy's outfit.

I keep a copy of Graham's on my nightstand. I propped up a pillow, flopped down in bed and turned on my reading lamp.

Then I drifted through the illustrations. Graham's Magazine was published during the 1840s and 50s and people subscribed because it had the latest in popular musical scores, stories, fashions, and art of the period.

When Edgar Allan Poe lived in Philadelphia, he worked for Graham's, and many of his stories and poems were first published in the magazine, which came out every month. If you were fortunate enough to subscribe to Graham's—and Graham's was found only in the best homes of the period—you were making a statement about your aesthetic values; that you valued art and culture and made a place for them in your life. It held appeal for those with aspirations and social ambitions.

After Poe died, Graham defended his character by writing articles in the magazine. He was a loyal friend. And now, it's like he's my friend too. When he talks about Poe, he talks to me, just me. I like this particular periodical because there are lovely pictures of village scenes, mothers and children, and moonscapes.

Every issue seems to have them. There are always dark, drifty clouds, twisted black trees, and gothic moons. One lithograph is called "Night Strangers" and it has several people in black cloaks moving along a moonlit road with wild leafless trees on each side, and they are on a journey somewhere. I was looking at it when I fell to sleep.


MYRON WAS LATE, yet everyone patiently chatted about their week while they waited for him to arrive. All the members came even though the weather was poor. There were thunderstorms most of the day.

He came in apologizing, saying he had to wait for traffic because of the rain.

"This is Myron, a professor at Dumphrey Community College," I announced, and went on to introduce him as a notable person who had an important poem accepted for publication in a respected magazine, and that soon his book will be published too, and everyone will know who he is, and that we should feel honored that he came to share his knowledge and his love of reading and literature with us.

Myron began by searching through his bag for something he wanted to read. He couldn't seem to locate it, and his hands were still wet and so was the bag, so when he finally found the letter, it was soggy.

It was a copy of a letter written by Oscar Wilde to his lover. He wrote it when he was in prison for loving this person. In it, he describes how he caused trouble for his family—his wife and their two sons—and it was out of the deepest sorrow and grief, just like in Psalm 130, and that's why it's called "De Profundis." He read the part where Oscar asks about how we might consider ourselves, our humanity.

> The final mystery is oneself. When one has weighed the sun in the balance, and measured the steps of the moon, and mapped out the seven heavens . . . there still remains oneself. Who can calculate the orbit of his own soul?

Everyone was quiet, like they were waiting for something, or maybe they were just beginning to suspect there was an unspoken connection among them.

Then Myron said, "Every person is the measure of the universe. What has meaning, if anything is to have meaning at all, must first have meaning to you, your center, or it will not be capable of meaning anything."

"I mean," Myron continued, "Even Picasso didn't see himself as the world saw him. To Picasso, Picasso was Picasso the poet, and did not think he would be remembered much as a painter. It is how Picasso saw his soul. And that is what is important."

I was waiting for him to get to the part where everyone would be happy reading the same book.

Instead, they asked Myron about his life, his thoughts, and what it was like to teach college, and what he read besides the letter by Oscar Wilde to his lover about his sadnesses.

It took the rest of the time we had left, but everyone, even Myron, seemed to have that indisputable and elevating sense of shared discovery.

I didn't know it then, but what happened that night was this: our book club, a readers' circle, morphed right into a writers' circle.

Mr. Nestor made a suggestion that put us on the path: we should read about what concerns us. And what was that? The things we experience and make an impression on us.

The others seemed to like the idea, so I said, "Let's write down the most important experience we can remember, then we'll read about ourselves to each other."

They all seemed pleased, maybe more than pleased, maybe a bit excited.


THE WEEK PASSED quickly and before we knew it, we were together again.

Everyone brought their own 'de profundis.'

Mr. Nestor volunteered to go first.

He wrote about how he loved his wife and how he never did enough for her, and when she died suddenly, he tried to kill himself with his tractor.

It didn't work. He drove up on the side of a hill on his farm, and kept the tractor at an angle until he tipped it over. The tractor would crush him.

But it didn't. It took him a week before he figured out how to do it right.

He had a new plan: he'd burn himself to death.

On his property, there's a natural cup in one of the fields and in the center is a stand of tall trees. He spent days hauling in all the dry wood he could find, and stacked it in a circle in the middle of the trees, then added bundles of straw soaked in gasoline, gallons of it. He stood in the middle and set it all on fire. He crossed his arms, waiting for eternity.

When the flames lurched towards him, and the black smoke billowed up all around, he had difficulty breathing, and the heat began to singe his skin. Then suddenly, the wind shifted.

A corridor opened through the smoke and led him out of his fiery circle. He knew his wife had made this happen because she wanted him to go on with his life and do things vital to himself and others.

That's when he decided to learn to read. It was something his wife always wanted him to do. Besides, then he could read his own IRS income tax forms, something his wife had been doing for years before she died.

When it was over, everyone clapped.

Jo-Jo cried.

There was a discussion. Everett compared Mr. Nestor to an action hero who survives uncommon danger so he may continue his quest. It was Everett's highest compliment. He turned to Mr. Nestor and said, "You are the questor."

The retired couple wanted to know his plans now that he had been saved. Sometimes they talk in unison, like they're twins. And they nod their heads too, at the same time, like when they were listening to Mr. Nestor, commiserating with him, who wants to write more about his wife and the farm they worked for 53 years because he knows everyone should remember the past like it's now because something tell us to do this, and the group agreed.

We had such a good session it went overtime.

Next week, Jo-Jo will read her 'de profundis.' She volunteered.

I was gathering my things when Mr. Bynes came by.

"Having a good night?" he asked, looking at me with his watery eyes.

"It was more than I expected," I said.

"Maybe I can join your group—next time."

"Sure. We can always add a member."

Then he switched the topic: "I've been working on the roof most of the day. You may have noticed." He was talking about a corner of the library building where the roof leaks. "I think it's patched up pretty good. There really isn't too much else to do at the moment, so I was wondering if I could fill in for the children's reader, only until she gets back, of course. I know it's not up to you, but maybe you could put a word in for me with Ms. Wills. I'm a good reader."

The children's reader, who had to leave early because of a sinus condition, is the older librarian. She wears a prairie dress on reading days, a granny-baby hat with ruffles, and sits in an oversized rocking chair. When she gets her sinus attacks, she's out for at least a couple of days.

OF COURSE MS. WILLS knew of the metamorphosis of our little group soon as it happened, like she's psychic.

I'm not a sneak. I didn't intentionally avoid going by her office the next day. It just turned out that way. Besides, even from where I was sitting at my desk which is some distance from her office, the presence of cumin was distinct.

So I got away with it. The next day too. But it couldn't go on forever. The third day was the one.

I was shelving some new acquisitions, murder mysteries. They're popular. People just seem to like murder mysteries. Ms. Wills picked up a title and pretended to examine it.

She was making me nervous, leafing through the pages like she expected to find something.

"You know, Frances," she began, "your book club is a reading group, not a *writing* group." She spoke deliberately, her voice low, and the words were pronounced with intensity. "A writing circle is not a reading circle. We must read before we write. That's the way of it. how can anyone write *before* they read? They need to understand something of the world first, and how human events occur. That means they must read about them. If they're encouraged to write, they just whine. Is that what you want, a whiners' circle?" and snapped the book shut, then set it back on the cart with the others.

She stood there for a moment, so I thought it might be a good time to change the subject. I asked if Mr. Bynes could fill in for our senior librarian who was out sick, and read to the children.

"Out of the question," Ms. Wills said.

She looked at her watch. "Why not stop by my office after lunch? We can talk a bit."

From that moment until after my lunch break, I was wondering if we were still on a first-name basis. Not that I would call her Blaonsch like she wanted, but the thought had crossed my mind. I tried to imagine myself saying it. I tried over and over, and I couldn't do it. It was bothersome, like Roxy's pink butterfly pageant costume. I don't know why that came to mind, but it did.

I was on my way to see Ms. Wills when my cell 'phone went off. I have it set to "vibrate" so I don't disturb the patrons, but no one seems to care about how much noise people make in the library, not like they used to. I still think it's important to respect others. Even though I don't make a point of asking people to lower their voices, I know the quieter it is, the more they can concentrate on what they're trying to think about, which is usually their books, or maybe something on the computer.

It was Myron. He had more good news. His chapbook, *Chances*, had just been accepted by *Ghost Moments Press*. Even though *Ghost Moments* is a small independent press, it's known for publishing really good poets with national reputations. Myron doesn't have a national reputation—not yet—and that's why he's so pleased. Soon as the book is out, he plans to apply for a National Endowment for the Arts grant. That's his next step. It's a big one and there's lots of competition.

"Generally speaking, in the life of a poet, the first book is considered the most important, certainly among bibliophiles. Somehow, it's precious, no matter how slight the actual volume may be," Myron said.

What happened when he informed his dean is even more amazing. The college wants him to head up its new honors program. The dean said they need someone like Myron to lead the way. He will become a director, and teach only two classes each semester. He will have an honors' scholarship fund, and a budget for recruiting, which means he can travel to high schools, and even have his own secretary.

"For all I know," he laughed, "an honors program could be a public relations move. The administration is always creating programs to increase student enrollment."

Even if that was true, what did it matter as long as students benefitted? Not to mention the fact that he would make the best honors director ever.

At this point, I imagined Myron blushing. It's really obvious when he does. I kid him about it, but not too much.

I know how authors feel about their books. I told Myron that an author should want at least one or two copies of his book in special collections. Special collections is not a repository immune to deaccession, but it's uncommon. They have some protection.

My secret is to be a librarian in special collections someday. Even if we had a special collections, I wouldn't want to work here. Not in Dumphrey. Somewhere else. But I don't have my certificate because I had to come home from grad school to look after Mama. Still, it's been my dream. I haven't told anyone, not Myron, not even my sister, Eva. That way, no one will be disappointed.

I talked with Myron for a long time on the 'phone and when I finally remembered I promised Ms. Wills I'd stop by her office, by the time I got there, the lights were off and her door was locked. She had gone home for the rest of the day.

There was a bibliography on my desk, left there to help me with my research on digitizing print journals. The new library assistant had looked up articles on the topic for me to help with my presentation in Philadelphia. It was kind of her. I wrote her a thank you note.

Later, I thought her leaving the bibliography was a hint. Maybe she wanted to go to the conference too. The bibliography was just her way of showing interest; to make herself part of the project. But that couldn't happen. There's barely enough in the budget to send one person, as it is. New librarians think that way though. They haven't heard about spending cuts year after year. You start thinking the library could close any time. I really don't believe that. I don't want to, anyway. But it wears on you. Librarians might not admit it, but it does, and the new librarians, even if they're part-time assistants, don't think that way because they haven't been hearing it for years. One thing, rumors of budget cuts keep the employees in line. They're not inclined to speak up as much, and they rarely grumble.

I made it a point to visit Ms. Wills first thing in the morning, and when I came in, I went directly to her office and waited while she finished up on her computer.

She clicked out of her file, pushed away from her desk, swung her chair around and asked, "Did you notice?"

I didn't know what she meant. "Notice . . . ?"

"The roof. The roof still leaks."

Ms. Wills looked at me with disgust.

It was her way of bringing up the subject of Mr. Bynes.

Apparently—and this wasn't long after he painted the walls all those bright and wonderful colors in the youth section of the library— Ms. Wills received a form from the state attorney general's office. It's a new requirement, sent to public service organizations, including the libraries, requiring them to begin monthly reports on registered sex offenders. Compliance is mandatory. There's some concern about offenders employed by the state and county regarding their job performance, behaviors, and so on. By requiring a report, administrators are expected to become more aware of their subordinates, and will be held more directly accountable.

Mr. Bynes has been here almost as long as I have. The hiring committee recommended him, but he would have been hired only if Ms. Wills approved because she has the final say.

"He seemed normal . . ." she said, drifting off, looking out the window as if something had happened she couldn't quite grasp.

"How could he have passed the screening process?" she wanted to know, then immediately answered her own question: "Human resources wasn't doing its job," she concluded. "They didn't do the proper back ground check, or if they did, they ignored it."

She looked pale and weak, which is rare. I've only seen Ms. Wills look this way once, and that's when she had a case of stomach flu.

"Can you imagine? *Nine* counts of child molestation?"

I couldn't. I couldn't imagine.

Ms. Wills had been thinking about her options. Her first impulse when she learned about his background was this: "I could fire him. I should, you know. I could do it too," she said. Then she reconsidered.

"Mr. Bynes might take legal action, and where would we be then? Everything would be out in the open, especially the question of why a library would have hired a child molester in the first place. It's too much to bear thinking about.

To make matters worse, Mr. Bynes actually comes from money, though you'd never expect it," she went on, "not by his career choice, anyway."

Ms. Wills explained that his family owned steel mills dating back to the Civil War, but Mr. Bynes was still considered a black sheep. "His family could step in, act on his behalf. You never know. He may not be the black sheep forever."

She went to the window, then motioned me to join her.

Mr. Bynes could be seen sweeping the walk below.

"Just look at him out there, a pedophile, for God's sake." She turned to me. "You must be more attentive now. Report anything suspicious, and keep him away from the children's section. I can't believe we've been working with a convicted felon."

We both looked at each other. We were both serious and stared at ourselves for the longest time, and then the oddest thing happened.

Ms. Wills' face relaxed. Her lips showed less tension, then a suggestion of a smile. It widened. Soon, she could no longer contain herself. She began to giggle.

She tried to stifle it with her hand, but it wouldn't go away. The more she tried to suppress it, the more amused I became just watching her, and before you knew it, there we were together, laughing out loud, laughing until we were both laughing so hard tears came to our eyes.

After things settled down, and we collected ourselves, I realized I could never look at Mr. Bynes in the same again. I wanted to think he may have overcome his problem.

Isn't that possible? After all, there's never been an incident since he's worked at the library. If something did occur, someone would find out about it, then everyone would know. That's how it works here in Dumphrey. Maybe things will be all right. I want to believe.

Ms. Wills informed me there's been a change to the conference program. I don't have to give a solo, standup presentation. I'll be on a panel with three or four other librarians who will talk about models for digitizing journals. What a relief! I may have to speak 20 minutes at most. Now I'll not have to research as much and I'll have time to do other things.

With all that's been going on, I almost forgot about our group meeting. I didn't prepare for it, but what was I supposed to do? They were all busy writing about their lives. Mr. Nestor added his first sequel to his original story. I suspect other members will do the same thing—adding other important events that happened to them, and sharing with the group.

Mr. Nestor waited for Jo-Jo. She brought copies of her most important experience and handed them out to the other members.

We followed along as Jo-Jo read to the group. She had been dating a popular boy at the high school, and talked about how much fun they had on their dates, and how much in love they were. When she became pregnant, she faced a big decision. Jo-Jo had to decide if she wanted to terminate her pregnancy, or go to term. If she had the baby, she didn't feel she could put it up for adoption.

When Jo-Jo decided to have the baby that's when her boyfriend joined the Navy. Now she's alone.

Usually the group will make comments, but this time no one said anything.

"Maybe we could return to Jo-Jo's story when we've all had time to think about it," I said. Everyone agreed.

We moved on to the couple. They wrote about each other; when they first met, and how they felt. They were at the county fair and were waiting in line for an amusement ride, the Tilt-A-Whirl. She was supposed to go on with a friend, but her friend was too scared, so she went on alone. She was all by herself in her car and the ride was about to start. All the other cars were full, and that's when she met her future husband.

The couple sat together and went 'round and 'round until they were dizzy. Later they had ice cream. They've been together ever since. But they never had children. They couldn't.

"Nature had other plans," they said.

This led back to Jo-Jo. They told her she was fortunate because she was having a child she wanted. "The worst thing," they said, "is to have a child you don't want. It's better not to have a child at all."

"It was a serious decision for me," Jo-Jo said. "It's the right thing for me to do, but I know girls in the program who didn't want their babies but they're having them anyway. I don't know why. Other girls, soon as they find out, decide not to, and that's all right because they wouldn't make good moms anyway. All my friends ask the same thing, 'how are you going to provide for the baby?' And I don't have the answer. I wish I did."

"Maybe your folks will help a little," someone said.

"I thought so. But they won't. I never thought they would be angry. I mean, they told me that if I was going to have it, I could just leave."

Jo-Jo seemed sad, maybe because she was sharing everything with the group. Her face was flushed, rosy-looking. She took out a

Kleenex and dabbed it around her eyes. "I'm sorry. I'm just embarrassed about it, that's all."

Everett said, "It's o.k. Sometimes pregnancy does that. Pregnant women glow," and looked down at his shoes. They're black, thick and scuffy, more like ankle boots with shoelaces.

She laughed a little, probably out of self-consciousness, or the attention she was receiving, but at that moment, everyone was happy for Jo-Jo.

After the others left, she stayed behind. I sensed she wanted to see me about something. She's well along—in her sixth month—and 'showing.' The other kids make fun of her in her classes. Teen moms had their own resource room at the high school, although with recent budget restrictions, they were 'mainstreamed' along with students with special needs; kids with physical disabilities, the learning disabled, all put into regular classes. She's teased constantly.

The next thing I knew she was in my arms. She pressed herself into me and spoke quietly into the hollow of my shoulder. "The only people who understand are the people in our group. We're all the same. We share our experiences by writing and reading and talking about them, and that's how we understand ourselves. It's how we manage the bad things. Otherwise, what would happen to us?'

While I was listening—I couldn't do anything but listen—I was struck by a rich mammalian odor so pervasive it was cloying. It was then I noticed my cheeks were wet.

"Don't," she said, "don't be sad, not for me."

I walked her outside. The couple was waiting for her in their car. They've been taking her to our meetings because Jo-Jo's parents won't let her drive the family car anymore.

We waved good-bye.

When my mother was pregnant, my grandmother knew it before she did. When Mama realized that she was, it turned into a family joke and everyone laughed about how grandma knew before Mama knew.

Sometimes I can detect it even among women who are older and had children years ago. It's one of those smells we never discover in ourselves, only in others. It's unmistakable.

I researched it once. The olfactory sense is the strongest and most memorable of all the senses of our species. It may not seem that way because we've developed a preference for sight. Over millennia, humans have suppressed smell, and at the same time, relied increasingly on their vision to make decisions, determine potential dangers, and identify objects of desire.

Some smells simply can't be tolerated. Horseradish—if I get too close to it—gives me a headache. Just peeling a garlic clove can trigger a gagging reflex.

My memory of high school is the memory of chlorine. Soon as I walked through the door, it washed over me in invisible waves. It was in the water. The staff cooked with it in the cafeteria. It came out of the drinking fountains. It ran from gym showers. And every night the school was cleaned with a solution mixed with chlorinated water.

When I came home, I swore it was in my clothes for hours. Even now, when I come to work at the library in the mornings, I know immediately if Mr. Bynes has been wiping down the floors or cleaning the furniture the night before.

The Dumphrey Water Treatment Department chlorinates recycled water over at the plant more than most other towns because our water has excessive bacteria. That's what the officials say. It's been that way since I can remember.

I like tarragon. It's one of my favorites. It should be French tarragon, freshly cut. It's the best. I use it in sachets. I make them myself and put them in with my things.

Cedar is special and it's in its own category. I keep a cedar cigar box my father used. Every once in a while, I open it and it reminds me of him. It's like he's become the essence of cedar.

THE INTERVENTION CAME when I least expected it. It happened when I was tucked away in the garage reading a biography of Sylvia Plath, and I was at the part where she's walking across the Cambridge quad on her way to meet Ted Hughes, her lover. Somehow, I was moving along with her, trying to keep up with her pace and I noticed her outfit. It was simple, and yet very becoming; a gray felt skirt and white blouse. Sylvia wore a light sweater thrown casually over her shoulders.

She had some books clutched to her chest. Maybe she had been reading and wanted to share her discoveries with Ted. Suddenly, she stopped and turned to me and tilted her head as if maybe she recognized me which of course was impossible.

Sylvia asked me if I was there for the interview. I was taken back, and I said yes even though it wasn't true, but I didn't know how else to explain being there, and this was an easy opportunity. Anyway, if Sylvia wanted to assume I was a reporter of some kind, why shouldn't I just go along with it?

I asked her, "Do you enjoy modeling?" since she'd been doing that lately. Modeling was fine with her but her real interest was in poetry, as I imagined it would be. It was clear she was in a hurry, and I didn't want to delay her.

"It's all right," she said, "I'm a bit early," and flipped her hair back and smiled. Her hair wasn't blond as I had seen in photographs, but darker. We chatted about her experiences at Cambridge although she seemed to want to talk more about Ted.

As she was going on with the most interesting conversation imaginable, Ms. Itsy was purring against my leg. I wasn't on the quad anymore. Ms. Itsy knew something was going on before I did.

There was a loud bang on the door. Then another.

**"FIRE DEPARTMENT. OPEN UP."**

By the time I reached the garage door, my ears were ringing, and the Chief was banging away like he wanted to break it down. When I opened the door, he was standing there with another fireman in their firemen's clothes with chartreuse neon stripes and all, and next to them was my sister Eva, Ms. Wills, and a building inspector from the town center along with someone from social services.

They all pushed themselves into the garage at once.

The Chief wanted to know when the structure was built. He called it a "structure," and I corrected him. I said it was a museum.

"Do you have a museum permit?"

"No, it's not that kind of museum," I said, and he moved past me along with the inspector.

Maybe I should have told him in French—*le musée imaginaire*—and skipped over the second syllable in *imaginaire*, like 'machk' in the back of my throat like Ms. Wills might do. Maybe it would have sounded more important. Maybe it wouldn't have been a "structure" then.

That might have impressed Ms. Wills, but something told me I wasn't going to impress the Chief no matter what I did.

It was the building inspector's turn: more questions: "How many electrical outlets do you have out here? Why? What's their purpose? Have you inspected them lately?"

"I read when it's dark."

He kept checking off boxes on a form attached to a clip board. Then he wrote down something and read it to me. There was a lot of official language, but basically, I was in violation of several building codes.

He had me sign it, then tore off a copy of the form and handed it to me.

I have 30 days to comply, or my garage will be closed and padlocked by the county with a "NO OCCUPANCY" sign on the door. Then it will go to a hearing to condemn the building.

"You do have a fire hazard here," the Chief said. "This isn't just about the failure to meet codes, it's about your own safety, Ms. Stryk." He pronounced it 'strike.'

The smell of steel hung in the air. I could hardly hear.

Ms. Wills was going from shelf to shelf surveying the books. "I never imagined anything like this," she said in a whisper, as if to herself, while turning 'round and 'round, appearing incredulous.

It was Eva's turn: "This is a tomb," she said, "that's what it is."

Then Eva asked the Chief, "How do we put an end to this? Even if the place is condemned, she'll go on hoarding. I just know she will. It's a disease."

"There's counseling available," Ms.Wills offered, and that's when the tiny woman from county social services pushed herself to the front. She's a social worker assigned to people like me who have "management issues," she said, smiling and trying to seem like she understood the situation.

She's probably the same person the county sends out to talk to people who have too many animals, or who stuff their houses with all kinds of junk. I tried to explain my book collection, but she didn't understand. If she really understood and saw things as I do, then she wouldn't have me to counsel.

What she did understand was that I needed "professional assistance," and gave me her card and a schedule for sessions she wanted me to go to. It was a group therapy program for people who have too much stuff that everyone else thinks is unnecessary for them to have, and having these things puts them in some kind of danger.

Everyone was waiting for me. They wanted me to agree with them so they could go on to the next person on their list.

I didn't agree to anything. Instead, I tried to get them to understand the importance of my collection and how carefully the books are arranged and how Myron put in hand-made shelves and that I had a fire extinguisher in the house—

Eva interrupted: "The house? The house if a fire trap too." She turned to the Chief, "You must inspect the house."

And they did.

They all marched off in a clump and went through my house. The inspector gave me another copy of another form. Same thing. Thirty days.

The last thing the Chief said was that my sister was right, and that all she wanted was for me to be safe. "You should thank her for alerting us," he said.

All I know is this: if I do what they want me to do, it will mean removing almost all of my books. They will no longer have a home and they will be lost forever.

After they left, I was exhausted. I went back to the garage and rested in the recliner for a while, thinking about all the commotion when I noticed Sylvia's biography still open on the little table next to the chair where I had left it. I tried to get back to where I was. I couldn't. I set the book down and closed my eyes and imagined peace.

I imagined floating. Relax, bones, I said. Peace, come and calm me, and I thought of tarragon. I imagined a basket of tarragon and thought about tarragon so much—sweet and fresh like a French field—the air became redolent with tarragon.

After a while, I began to feel better, and eventually I was able to pick up the book and soon as I did, there was that immense green field at Cambridge and I was with Sylvia again just like nothing had happened, and there was never a moment's interruption.

We spoke about her ambitions; how she would become a famous poet. She knew this would happen. Then I asked about her family, mainly her father, a beekeeper and a scholar who wrote a book on bees, whom she loved dearly, but many people, years later, after they read her poem, "Daddy," wouldn't think so. They would think Sylvia believed her father was a brutal man, especially when she compared him to a vampire, and a fascist, and finally called him a "bastard."

We both stopped walking. Sylvia turned to me and looked appalled. She swore she would never do such a thing.

I knew that one day she would have another interview, a real one, and she would be asked about "Daddy" and she would be coy and elusive and treat the entire subject of her father in the poem dismissively, and pretend to be amused that anyone would think her poem portrayed her father as an evil person.

I didn't tell her that after that interview, she would take her life four months later. For now, she wanted to see Ted, and I didn't want to detain her any longer. I wanted to say that she was headed for trouble with Ted, that he would leave her for another woman, and later during one of London's coldest winters, she would roll up towels and seal the door of her apartment, and squeeze them under the door that led to the bedroom where her children were sleeping, and turn on the gas and put her head in the oven and leave her babies in the next room without their mother forever.

The breeze was picking up and our talk began to dissolve the way images do when they began to fragment and fall away, and I could see that she was disappearing, and when she was gone there would be nothing left, nothing but the odor of sanctity.

Except for my mother, I'd never seen anyone die. When my mother died, I didn't smell anything because my nose was stuffed up from crying. Some say when saints die their bodies give off a floral scent that lingers for days. The odor of cut flowers is much too heady, even when there are only a few. No, this was something more refined.

The odor of sanctity is the scent of sunlight.

When my mother died, she was in hospice. Cancer. It started somewhere—they were never quite sure—and spread all over. By the time she was diagnosed, most of her organs were in some stage of degeneration. Hospice was the most humane thing to do; at least that's what everyone said.

She was on "No Code," which means she couldn't be resuscitated no matter what. The medical staff set up a morphine drip so she could self-medicate. Whenever she became conscious of pain, she could push a white plastic plunger. Sometimes you knew she was in pain but she too weak to push the plunger.

So I helped her. Then it kept wearing off. She needed more and more. The amount was set so she wouldn't overdose.

Once when we were visiting her, she asked for water, and we were prevented from giving it to her. I even asked the nurse if Mama could suck on an ice cube. The nurse said this was impossible, and explained the patient must be able to take food or water on her own, otherwise it was considered an uncommon attempt to sustain life and that wasn't in the medical papers Mama signed. It came under the "No unusual, heroic, or exotic treatment" part. Another thing the nurse wanted us to know was this: Mama could not be given too much morphine because she could become addicted. It took her a month to die. When I visited, all I could hear was her moaning. She died of starvation.

That's the way it happens in hospice. You die of starvation. Eva said she never wanted to die like our mother did.

EVERETT WAS NEXT. He works in a comic shop. It's the only one in town. He leases it, and as the owner of the business, he buys and sells through his own website, online auctions as well as over-the-counter. He announced the latest X-Man comic book had just arrived. He has them piled on his counter. "Hot sellers," he said.

The group listened attentively, but no one said anything.

Everett read from his notebook. His most important experience was when he discovered action heroes. Before that time, he wasn't much interested in them. He remembered the exact day when he discovered his heroes. He was home from school with a sore throat, and some men in uniform came to the door and spoke with his mother. After they left, she came over and sat at Everett's bedside for the longest time. Then she cried, and through her crying told Everett that his father, who had been serving in Operation Iraqi Freedom, wouldn't be coming home.

That was Everett's 'de profundis.' The next episode, he promised, will be how his father was like a super-hero, and how someday, Everett might write his own comic book about him.

We were done: everyone had read about their most important experience and now they were onto sequels.

Everyone was waiting for something. I sensed it was coming, and I should have expected it and prepared for it, but I didn't.

Finally Jo-Jo said, "Everybody has shared their most important experience, everybody but *you*."

The members chimed in: yes, they wanted me to read my story to them, but I wasn't ready. After all, I'd been working on my research paper, and trying to figure out what to do with my books and the wiring in my house and my garage, and besides, I never expected anyone to ask. That's what I told them.

"Maybe next time," I said, hoping there would never be a next time.


SATURDAY, EVA HAD MORE tax work with clients and asked if I'd look after Roxy. I agreed to take her to the movies, some Walt Disney fantasy Eva wanted Roxy to see. A matinée.

Instead, we went to a girls' softball game. Some of Roxy's friends were playing. My niece tried out once, and made the cuts, but Eva wouldn't let her play. In fact, Eva was upset with me for having taken

Roxy to the try-outs in the first place. It took weeks before we were on speaking terms again, and another month before she'd even let me see Roxy.

Before I left the house, I took Roxy's jeans, threw in a sweatshirt, and on my way out, grabbed a bag of stale bread I'd been saving.

After the game, the team was going to the Dairy Barn to get shakes and ice cream. They invited Roxy to come along.

I waited in the car.

Afterward, we drove to the park and walked down to the pond to feed the ducks. Roxy loves this. The ducks are aggressive and come right up and peck at your feet if you don't feed them. It makes her laugh.

Among the ducks floating around in the pond, there were two black swans. They have orange bills and always swim alongside one another. No one knows where they came from. They just flew in late one spring and never left.

We bought a sub from a vendor and took it to a bench by the pond. We shared it, but most of the bread went to the ducks.

Roxy winced when she looked at me. "I want a tattoo."

I wanted to tell her that most people have tattoos. Invisible ones. If they could be read, those tattoos would say "I belong to X," and X would be someone, or something. Throughout history, slaves were tattooed. People walk through their entire lives being slaves to other people or things. I didn't want that for Roxy.

Instead, I said, "Do the other girls have them? The girls on the team?"

"Some do. But they hide them so their parents don't see."

"What kind of tattoos do they have?"

"Bad ones. They tattoo themselves."

"What kind of tattoos do you like?"

"I dunno."

"Well, if you were to get a tattoo, what kind of tattoo would you get?"

"Ummmm. A duck," and she laughed.

The black swans drifted over.

"Do you know," I said to Roxy, intentionally changing the subject, "for a very long time, people believed there weren't any black swans. All swans were white swans."

Roxy laughed, "I want to swim with them! I want to swim with the swans!"

We both laughed together. Everything was good that day.


HE JUST DROPPED IN, took a chair, and asked, "Do you mind if I sit in with the group?"

I told him about the rule: you have to write, then read, your most important experience, and that's just for starters. You have to be willing to discuss it too, and he nodded. I introduced Mr. Bynes to each of the members. Funny, I didn't know his first name—

"Ward," he said, and removed a couple of sheets from a manila folder and held them up. "As you can see, I came prepared."

I just knew he was going to tell us about child molestation. I tensed up thinking it was coming. It was just my own apprehension. It wasn't what I imagined. Mr. Bynes had written about his home life, when he first realized he had been abandoned.

His father committed an "indiscretion" with a younger woman. The result was Mr. Bynes. His father's family found out—mainly his father's wife—and she was not happy, not one bit.

When he was six, he remembers it exactly, he was left alone. His mother went out and never came back, just like that. He remembers the apartment where she left him, all the details, the color of the blinds, the carpet, even pieces of furniture.

He waited a long time, then he went outside to see if she might be coming down the street, and when he didn't see her, he decided to wait in a vacant lot next door. He sat on the ground for hours, and just before nightfall, a stranger out walking a dog, called the local police. That's how he was rescued.

Ward's father wanted to take him in to live with his family, but his wife was against it and refused to discuss it at all. When it became apparent the boy wouldn't be accepted by the family, he was sent to live with an elderly aunt, a spinster, who not only kept the money sent to her for Ward's support, but sent him out to work early. She took what pay he made telling him he had to learn to support himself. She claimed, until the day she died, no one had ever given her anything for Ward, and that she was penniless.

"Sounds like something out of Dickens," Everett said.

Everyone ignored him except Jo-Jo who tried to keep herself from giggling.

"Go on with the story," Mr. Nestor said.

"Yes, do," the couple agreed.

Mr. Bynes went on about his boyhood, about how he worked such long hours his school work suffered and he became so discouraged, he dropped out of high school soon as he could to work full-time for a security company that sold and installed concertina wire, burglar alarms, and put up cages around parking lots.

"It wasn't even a childhood, I mean, who could call it that?" he asked.

He had to work ever since he dropped out of school, and the fact he had been abandoned never left him. He thinks about it every day. "No child should have to worry about that, or having real parents, or a place to sleep at night," he said.

Mr. Nestor, who had his head down as if he might be resting, perked up and said, "Things we've had become greater than they ever were when they're taken away. Some experiences, like childhood, can never be recovered, and the more we think about it, the bigger the loss becomes."

Mr. Bynes said, "For sure."

"You must have a lonely life," the couple said.

Mr. Bynes shrugged his shoulders. "Only if I think about it. But if I keep myself busy and stay uplifted, it's not so bad."

Everett wanted to know what Mr. Bynes meant by "uplifted."

"When I stay positive."

"How do you do that?" Everett asked.

"I think good thoughts."

"All the time?"

"I try."

"I see."

Jo-Jo spoke up. "It's hard to overcome an empty childhood."

Before we broke up, someone asked if we could make copies of our writing, and keep them together. We could add to them as we went along.

"Like an anthology," Everett said. "The stories of ourselves are really the stories of other people too. It's what we're made of."

I TRIED TO GET THE GROUP to refocus, get them writing and reading new stories about their lives, but they were intent on getting me involved.

It couldn't happen because I hadn't written anything and you had to write something to read to the group and that was the rule.

"Then tell us," they all said at once.

Mr. Nestor said, "Frances, you're part of our group too. We've all shared ourselves, haven't we? Now it's your turn."

"I'd be breaking the rule."

Jo-Jo said, "We've taken a vote and we voted for an exception, so you're the exception now."

They all stared at me. Maybe I could do this quickly if I spoke fast.

"All right," I said. "Here goes." First, they had to understand this about my family: Eva is several years older and there were just the two of us growing up. Mama was a lot younger than Daddy when they met. After they married, he worked himself up to an assistant manager at Dumphrey Mining and Manufacturing and he had something like 25 years with the company and we were doing fairly well.

Soon as I was old enough to be in school and Mama didn't have to stay home, she took a job as a secretary and there was enough money coming in to buy Eva her own piano and to pay for private piano lessons, but she never did much with it even though our parents encouraged her.

When Daddy lost his job because the mine closed, he seemed to have accepted it as one of those things that just happen, and to make the best of it. He took it in stride. He still loved music, and he still danced with me. That's what I remember most about him, how he had a good disposition. Eva disagrees.

Eva doesn't remember him dancing. Not with me. Not with anyone. She said he was "grim." So we disagree about our dad. It never occurred to me that he might be grim. To me, he was always playful. I think he played with me more than anyone.

About a year after he was laid off, we had to start selling things; family heirlooms, household items, the car, everything but Eva's piano. Mama worked overtime to keep paying the bills and the mortgage.

One afternoon, Eva and I came home from school, and when we got off the bus, Daddy wasn't there to meet us, and that never happened. He was always there.

When we got home, the house was so quiet you could feel it. We called for him and there was no answer. We went through every room in the house.

Then we went down to the cellar. He'd work on wood projects down there—foot stools, birdhouses, things like that—and he had a little tool bench in one corner with a radio. It was set to a classical station. FM. It was still playing.

Eva and I disagree on our memories. But I remember it clearly. It's one of those images that never goes away. This was my 'de profundis,' my moment of greatest sorrow. Just remembering it, and certainly, speaking about it, is as if I am reliving the event all over again. It doesn't go away.

Eva says we both saw our father hanging from a beam. It wasn't a surprise to Eva because she always thought he was "grim" anyway, and she expected something like this would happen someday.

He was sitting by his workbench with the things about him that he loved, slumped over and listening to the music playing on the radio.

Eva said, "Daddy can't be listening to music. He can't be listening to anything because he's dead."

It was *Beethoven's Piano Concerto Number 3*. I remember it because the announcer mentioned it at the end of the program. Other works in that program included Samuel Barber's *Adagio for Strings*, and Erik Satie's *Gymnopédie Number 1*. To this day, these are my favorite musical compositions.

Eva grabbed me and pulled me around. She pointed to the ceiling, but there was nothing there. Just the beams. I remember too, the smell of his cigar smoke; bitter and obstinate. It wouldn't leave.

Even today, the cellar smells of cigar smoke. It was absorbed in the rafters and in the walls. It's there all right, and it didn't matter that Eva had the cellar cleaned with disinfectant by a professional cleaning service.

When mother died and left the house to Eva, she moved everything out of the cellar and re-plastered the walls white. There's nothing there now, just empty space, and of course, the smell of Daddy's cigar. Not a piece of furniture, not Daddy's workbench, nothing. I asked for the radio once, but Eva said it was sold in the estate sale. She put everything she didn't want in a pile, and had some estate sale company come over and sort out the items, then put price tags on them. When Eva had the sale she never told me about it.

Anyway, there's nothing in the cellar now. It's just a cold, damp, empty place. My sister keeps it that way. If only Eva would let me store my books there, it would be an improvement, that's for sure.

But I know better, and I don't talk to her about it anymore.

The members of our writers' circle all nodded as if they understood and smiled kind smiles.

THE NEXT DAY WAS SATURDAY, and I drove over to a recreational store to pick up some things I'd need for the Philadelphia trip. I needed a new pair of hiking boots because mine are just about worn through, some socks, and a bandana so my hair doesn't blow into my face. I'd have picked up something for Roxy, but I have to be selective, and not do it too often either, or Eva objects.

When I was driving back home, coming down my block, I saw someone waiting on my front porch.

It was Jo-Jo. She was holding something. A box. Soon as I climbed up the steps she presented it to me.

"Here," she said, "I baked it myself." She flipped back the top so I could see.

It was a fruit pie.

I was about to take it, and she withdrew, took a step back. She looked at me like she was suspicious.

"Wa—ait a minute," she said. "There's something on your mind."

I removed my glasses. "What makes you think that?"

"Intuition. It's like you're worried about something."

I think I might have clicked my glasses—maybe—once or twice.

"No, nothing," I assured her.

"Let me guess then?"

"Sure."

"Philadelphia is coming up, right?"

"Right."

"And you'll be gone for a few days, right?"

Actually, I'd be gone for a good week. I'd taken a couple of extra vacation days so I could spend more time in the city and do some of the things I've been wanting to do.

"Let me guess: you're worried about your house and your books and you don't want to leave them, am I right?"

She was, especially since I hadn't figured out what to do about my electrical problem, and was concerned about that too.

"Why not let me house sit?" she asked. "I'm really good at that, and I'd be happy to do it for you."


PHILADELPHIA WAS MARVELOUS. I don't know why I just don't move there. Well, I do know why, because I don't have a job in Philadelphia. I have a job in Dumphrey. Besides, what's left of my family is in Dumphrey.

The panel session was one of the best. The conference attendees said so. Part of my presentation on digital conversions was taken from personal experience. It was the last part of my talk, about the necessity of electronic transfers, and it involved Myron, and even though it happened a few years ago, this kind of thing still goes on today, probably more than ever, so it's relevant. That's what I said.

A new administrative team came to Myron's community college and appointed several people they knew to staff positions. They imported them from other colleges because they knew them very well and they could trust them and they all shared the same views and would carry out administrative mandates, one of which was to create extra space without erecting a new building.

The college always needs more space. The new director of library services at Dumphrey Community College was the first to suggest taking the music room and converting it to an office for the new vice-president of assessment and evaluation who didn't have an office.

Plus, it was a perfect excuse to get rid of the music room. It was just one less place for students to "loiter." That's what the administration said. In fact, students never loitered there at all. They loitered other places.

Myron thinks the president came up with the idea, then told the new director of library services to act like she came up with it. That way, if anyone was unhappy, he wouldn't get blamed for it.

The music room had been around since the college opened. Students could go there and listen to foreign language tapes, musical recordings, and there were several record players with individual carrels, headphone sets, and shelves upon shelves of LPs.

Most of the holdings can't be found any longer: Native American songs released in limited editions prior to 1950—not only those indigenous to the northeast, but chants and the ritual music of plains' nations—an extensive collection of French opera albums bequeathed by a Jesuit who retired to our town so he could live with his sister, the original Caedmon recordings of poets reading their own poems: Dylan Thomas, T. S. Eliot, and Gertrude Stein to name a few. There were recordings of the Charles Eliot Norton Lectures, including readings by several notable literary figures. Other recordings included classical, pop, jazz, and secular scores.

In all, there were over 700 items.

When Myron learned what was to be done with the holdings of the music room he had just returned from teaching and it was late in the afternoon. Soon as he put his briefcase on his desk and began removing papers, his 'phone went off.

It was the secretary who worked in his department, and knew Myron's fondness for the music room, its contribution to students' lives, and the riches it contained.

On the way out of the building where the music room is located, she noticed recordings stacked in the hallway. Each had a clear archival liner and they were piled horizontally, on top of one another, which is the worst way to place them. The weight damages the grooves, and the vinyl warps. They should be stored vertically, on their edge, just like books, pressed firmly together, but not tight either, just so they won't bend and may be easily removed, and returned.

The secretary asked one of the librarians why the albums were piled up in the hallway, and she was told they were there "for the taking." Anyone could have them. They had been deaccessed.

Apparently, the library director—at the direction of the administration—tried to sell them locally, but without results. They just wanted them out of the building so they could move ahead with their office plan. If the recordings were not taken away by the end of the following day, they would be thrown out.

Soon as the secretary finished telling Myron about the albums, he was in his car, driving over to the college. Once he saw the stacks in the hall, he went directly to the president's office. He was lucky because he managed to catch the president just as he was leaving his office for a trip to another campus.

Myron told him of the value of the collection as they walked across the parking lot toward the president's car.

"Value," the president said, "is a relative term. If these things have any value, then find a place for them. We can't. The demand for office space is too great."

When Myron protested, the president said something that ended their conversation. He said, "These can be replaced with electronic files. They're all available, right? And we will do that just as soon as possible. You can count on it."

Of course, they could not be replaced, and not one—not the president, or any other administrator—ever made the effort to do so.

The last thing Myron said was, "The cultural history of America is being lost," and with that, the president drove away.

Myron and the music teacher met in the hallway and divided up the albums. The music teacher took many of them, and Myron asked Ms. Wills at the library if she would take the rest. She declined saying, "No one that I know of would want to listen to any of them. We know what our patrons need. They tell us. And we've never had requests for any of those items."

Myron kept quite a few, and shared some with me. These are shelved in my spare bedroom at home. They take up an entire wall.

The other panelists clapped when I was done telling them the story about how precious materials can be lost. We all went out for dinner.

Every night, I emailed Ms. Wills about what I did at the conference, even though she never asked me to. I thought she'd be interested.

ON MY LAST DAY, I took the afternoon off and drove to the Wissahickon. It was like I remembered it when I was a student. I strapped on my new hiking boots and from the entrance by the landing, followed the path down to the stream, then all the way up to the Valley Green Inn and had a blueberry cobbler. It wasn't an ordinary cobbler; it was eighteenth-century size, which means it's served hot in a bowl. There was so much of it, I couldn't eat it all.

On my way back, I switched to the other side of the stream so I could go by Rinker's Rock where Edgar Allan Poe saw the great elk, and later wrote about it, and before that, where soldiers marched during the Revolutionary War, and before that, where the Lenape hunted their game. The path is worn.

Instead of driving back the next morning, I visited the rare book room and special collections at the Philadelphia Free Library. I couldn't leave the city without doing that.

On my visit, I made a new friend. I was looking over the art book exhibit. Some of these books don't even have words, they're just unique shapes and colored images and made out of all kinds of material; what people find. Odds and ends. Ms. Wills calls them *objets de rebut*. One was made from the pages of a telephone directory and it was shaped like a cone, a space capsule, or something. There was a series of leather covers stitched together with copper wire. They were stained with various shades of indigo, stained right into the leather like Rorschach splotches, so they suggest whatever image you are able to imagine. They're kept in archives just like in an art museum, but they're in special collections in the library.

There was someone next to me, and remarked about how the art books are fascinating, and I agreed. We chatted a little, and when she learned I was there for the librarians' conference, she offered to show me other items that were being put together for an exhibition.

I was still in my hiking clothes, and I didn't look anything like a librarian ought to look, and I felt uncomfortable, so I tried to explain myself.

I mentioned I had just been to Rinker's Rock where Poe saw the great elk from his skiff, and that he wrote about it in his famous essay about the Wissahickon, and how I followed the stream on foot.

"You must be fond of Poe then?"

I said I loved Poe even though Harold Bloom called him a "bad poet," and Harold Bloom is an important critic with a prodigious literary intelligence, but I can't help it, I have to disagree with Mr. Bloom.

She seemed amused by what I said, then led me upstairs, down a long hallway to a cramped room with one tiny window, and asked me to wait. The room had mahogany paneling so dark it was nearly black, and there was a long table pushed up against a wall with a book cradle.

A few minutes later, she returned with a presentation copy of Poe's "The Raven," written in his own hand on thin, bluish paper. It was the poem that made him famous around the world. His handwriting is nearly perfect. All the letters are formed precisely. You could measure the length of the loops in the 'g's for example, and they would be the same.

She let me examine the manuscript without gloves or anything. After seeing that I was taken with the poem and Poe's writing, she left again, and came back with a copy of *Tamerlane*, Poe's first little book. It's a pamphlet really, like Myron's chapbook, except the cover isn't made of card stock, it's the same thin paper as the pages.

There are only twelve copies known to exist, she told me, and among book collectors, it's known as "The Crown Jewel of American Literature."

"Poe published it himself, and it didn't cost much, maybe 15 cents a copy. He just paid the printer. Many of our best writers did this," she added, "mainly when they were starting out."

The last item was a small glass vial, maybe crystal, with etched sides and a glass stopper.

It had to be special. In fact, most libraries, if they're lucky enough to have things like this, don't list them in their public catalogue, or they would be pestered by curiosity seekers, and the librarians would never get any work done.

I knew I was getting unusual treatment, and that was fine with me. Maybe it was because I was a librarian too, I thought.

"This vial," she said, "belonged to Virginia, Poe's wife."

I was so astonished, I could hardly believe it. I asked if I could remove the stopper, and her eyebrows went up yes. When I passed it under my nose, just once, I could detect the faint scent of lavender, probably from the dry residue along the sides of the bottle.

She asked, "Can you smell anything?"

"Of course not," I said, "it's much too old, a century and a half at least. How could I?"

She smiled. "I can."

"You can?"

"Yes."

"What do you smell?" I asked.

"Oh . . . . maybe a hint of lavender."

That's when I knew we would be friends.

Her name is Dana. We exchanged cards. I wasn't going to tell her my secret about wanting to work in special collections, but when I went on saying how grateful I was that she showed me these things, and how I admired people like her, it kind of came out. I said, "I really want to be like you."

Before I left, I gave her two copies of Myron's chapbook. He signed them like I asked him to.

Dana looked them over and noticed Myron's biographical note on the back cover. "I see you're from the same area," she said, meaning Dumphrey. She probably suspected we were friends too.

Dana promised to keep them "safe," and called them "a contribution to our special collections" which would make Myron proud, and it's something I'll tell him about when I get home.

She gave me a form letter saying the books had been gifted to the library, then I signed it as the donor, and that made it official.

When I left, she put out her hand, "Let's stay in touch."

Before leaving Philadelphia, I made a quick trip over to the Redding Market by the train terminal and looked around for presents. I wanted to get something for Eva, and Roxy, and Jo-Jo for house sitting and watching over my books and for taking care of Ms. Itsy.

In the Amish booth I found some quilted hand-made pot holders with Dutch designs. They would be good for Eva.

It took more time to find Roxy's gift. There was a jewelry stand with a nice selection of earrings and bracelets. Most were silver and had little enameled flowers. I found a matching set. But I didn't buy it; instead I bought Roxy something else. I brought her a bracelet. A leather one.

As for Jo-Jo, there was a dry goods booth near the exit, and I picked up a baby quilt. It had an interesting pattern with many colors so it wasn't a boy quilt or a girl quilt. It was just a baby quilt.

MY MIND WAS WANDERING on the drive back. I was thinking about Dana and what she had done for me—showing me those priceless things—and she reminded me of another tall, calm and thoughtful person, the person my mother told me about when she read to me when I was a child. So when I am remembering Dana, I'm remembering Dame Consolation.

For more than a thousand years everyone knew about Dame Consolation. She was the figure of wisdom in Boethius' *The Consolation of Philosophy*. Boethius was imprisoned when she appeared to him. She told him about what fame really is, and time, and identity, and why we shouldn't worry. No one reads Boethius anymore, not now anyway. For hundreds of years, schoolchildren memorized passages right from the book. Even when my own mother was in school, they were reading Boethius.

Mama once won a prize for memorizing the passage about fame, how if we live 10,000 years and your name is known, it's nothing against the largeness of eternity.

Kids today don't learn about Boethius. I bet their teachers never heard much about him either. So for me, if there were ever a real Dame Consolation, it would be Dana.

Her clothes probably carry the scent of sunlight.

I COULDN'T WAIT to tell Myron about my experiences in Philadelphia, and when I finally did, he had some news for me too.

We met for lunch. The college has a nice cafeteria, and it takes me about five minutes to drive over from the library. The food isn't as bad as most school cafeterias, and the prices are reasonable.

Myron has a friend, an attorney who works for the county, who told Myron he could get an extension for me on my fire violations if I just repair my electrical wiring and outlets "to bring them up to code." Also, Myron found out about a contractor who worked on the attorney's office when it was being built, and he arranged for him to come over and take a look at my house, which is a good thing because my 30 days is almost up.

I was really grateful to Myron for what he did, and then—this was even better—he spread out a copy of *The Dumphrey Democrat and Chronicle.*

The Writers' Circle had composed a letter to the editor without my knowing. When it was finished, they asked Myron to proof read it for them. It just happened to come out in the newspaper when I was away in Philadelphia. Myron saved a copy.

> Dear Editor,
>
> We want everyone to know that The Writers'
> Circle that meets over at the library has changed
> our lives. We all feel this way. Ms. Stryk conducts
> our meetings. She is smart and sensitive and patient,
> and we (the under-signed) are glad she's doing this.
> Also we want to thank the Dumphrey County Library
> for its willingness to offer this educational opportunity
> to the residents of Dumphrey. We speak all for one,
> and each speaks for the other one when we say our

experience is like finding a family, one we should have found in the first place, but didn't.

It was signed by everyone in the group, all five.

Myron, who knows I've been having some disagreements with Ms. Wills about our writing circle, tapped the page with his pen and said, "no one should be criticizing you now," and smiled. "In fact, it wouldn't surprise me if Ms. Wills wanted more writers' circles after this." Then Myron talked and talked about his new job as the honors director. Unfortunately, he didn't have it very long. It was taken away from him, and he doesn't know what else might happen, and it's all because of his book he wanted so much to publish.

*Ghost Moments Press* is in trouble. In a letter from its publisher to another young poet, it was noted that the press was under financial pressures, and as much as *Ghost Moments* would like to publish the poet's submission, the press had to use what funds it had to bring out books by a few other poets, like Myron, and some high-end critical essays. In his letter, the publisher did suggest the possibility of a co-operative venture, where the poet would contribute to perhaps a third of the cost of bringing out a collection.

The poet was young and anxious, and one day did not pass until he took to the social media and denounced *Ghost Moments* as a vanity press, which just isn't true. At the time, there were several other *Ghost Moments* authors who had submitted for various grants, using their books as publication credits. In addition, their *Ghost Moments* books had, in many cases, either contributed to their tenure, or were directly responsible for the writers achieving academic advancement. The National Endowment for the Arts, soon as they learned of the young poet's allegations, deemed *Ghost Moments* a subsidy press, and eliminated any consideration of authors who had books with the press. As for Myron, by his association with the press—just having published *Chances*—made him ineligible for the grant he wanted so much. When the college learned about this, they removed him from his position as honors director. It's amazing how ready people are to believe what isn't true.

I remembered my recent conversation with Dana, and how she said Poe published his own poetry at first. I thought of other authors too, like Walt Whitman, and Virginia Woolf, and Ezra Pound. It all seemed unfair. Myron hadn't done anything wrong. He hadn't subsidized his book, or financed it in any way. But that didn't stop the college from saying that he had. They didn't send him a letter or anything, they just called him in and told him the administration had decided not have an honors director for a while, and that a dean would add the program to his list of duties.

"So that's that," Myron said. "The student literary society had invited me to give a reading, but as of this morning, they cancelled, and the student newspaper wants an interview before they write an editorial opinion."

"Will you give it to them?"

"I'm still thinking about it. It could make matters worse."

"Maybe you should tell them the facts. You could be vindicated. Why don't you try it?"

We made our way to the cafeteria buffet line, and picked up a tray.

"As it stands, I can go on teaching basic composition classes. I don't want to do anything that would jeopardize that. A defense, even if just, may be frowned upon by the same administrators who already made their decision."

We placed some fruit cups on the tray, a tuna salad sandwich that we'd share, and iced tea.

"It's like having a contagious disease," he went on, "no one wants to be around you. I honestly don't think I should ever again be able to place anything with magazine or book publishers with integrity. They will not want to associate with me simply because they would be aligning themselves with a black-listed publisher. Once something like this picks up in the national literary community, there's no stopping it. People will agree with just about any travesty simply to advance themselves by lining up with the others, the ones who've condemned the publisher and could never change their minds once they made their condemnation."

He was pale and seemed distracted. I wanted to tell him that the two copies of his new book are now in the special collections department of the Philadelphia Free Library, which is a very fine thing, but he didn't look like he would appreciate it, not now anyway. Maybe later.

He worked so hard for so many years on his chapbook, and I think what's happening, what he's going through, is his 'de profundis.'


THE UNFORTUNATES. That's what Mama called them. They are people who lose their jobs, or their homes, or always seem to be down on their luck, or had some tragedy in their lives.

"You never want to be an unfortunate," she would tell me. "Be self-sufficient and you will never have to ask other people for what's not yours to begin with."

That's why Eva became an accountant. Maybe that's why I became a librarian, but with me, it's more than that. The books mean more than just about anything, so I could never be away from them for very long even if I wanted to.

I never thought Mama would be an unfortunate. But that's what happened. Her problems began with Daddy just leaving us in the cellar the way he did, then a couple of years later, Mama was diagnosed with cancer and I moved back home to care for her until it was time for hospice. It just got worse, and after a few months, she died.

I never thought Eva would be an unfortunate. Eva has what Mama had. She went in to see her doctor because she was tired all the time, and the last cold she had lasted forever. They took a blood sample, and the next thing I knew, she had "irregularities," that's what her doctor said. They examined some cells and they found Eva has leukemia.

No one knows about it. When I took over the Amish pan holders I bought in Philadelphia, Eva told me in confidence. Roxy doesn't have a clue. She just knows her mother's tired a lot.


I'VE BEEN LIVING at Eva's house ever since they took a bone marrow sample, then put her on drug therapy, though no one's optimistic. I drive Eva to the care center for transfusions every few days now, and I take care of Roxy, and do the laundry and shopping, while still working at the library and keeping up with the writers' circle.

Trying to help Mama was the hardest thing I ever had to do. I don't know if I can go through it again. I even tried to donate blood for Eva's transfusions, but I can't. I'm not her type. The lab tech told my doctor and my doctor told me and I told Eva, then Eva called my doctor to make sure.

Eva complains. I think she should remain calm and not upset herself. She really doesn't want me in the house, but she's the one who asked me to be with her in the first place, after she became so weak she couldn't do much.

She's allergic to Ms. Itsy. That what she says anyway. Of course, Roxy loves the cat and thinks we are all finally together like we should have been years ago. I try to keep Ms. Itsy away from Eva as much as I can. Bringing my cat to live in Eva's house isn't helping her attitude like I thought it would.

One afternoon, I took some tea up to Eva. She was sitting on the edge of her bed.

"You'll have to take of Roxanne," she said.

"You mean . . . ."

"I mean exactly what I said. You will have to care for her. Who else would?"

"That's a long way off, besides there's still hope," I said because she's been taking some new chemo treatments and maybe something magical will happen. Sometimes it does. You hear about it. A terminal case will recover and no one knows why.

Eva shook her head no.

"Here," she said, "reaching over to open the top drawer of her night stand. "Take this."

It was a plain envelope.

"Inside is everything you will require. After—" she stopped, and made a motion as if pushing back her hair, a habit, except now there's just a few wisps, and sighed, "after it's all over, you can go through it. There's everything you need for Roxanne."

Pretty soon Eva will go into hospice too, just like Mama. It's the same one. I can't keep this up. She's just getting worse. The liaison person at the hospital is convinced that Eva's going through stages. Right now, she's grumpy. That will pass though, and then she will become accepting. That's what happens to unfortunates. Their luck gets so bad, they don't try any more. Mama used to say, "You can't win for losing."

Ms. Wills lets me have more time to take care of Eva, only when I really have to, which is becoming more and more often. I hope she gets in hospice soon. Eva gets evaluated every week. If the evaluation team says it's time to go to hospice, then she can go.

It's good I can still meet with the writers' circle. When we have our night sessions, Myron fills in for me at the house; he takes care of Eva, and watches over Roxy until I get back.

The other night, Mr. Nestor was reading about how his wife has been appearing to him in her dreams, and how they have conversations just like they had when she was alive. They mostly talk about the farm, and what needs to be done, and that Mr. Nestor is saving his receipts so he can do his own taxes for the IRS.

Everett said Mr. Nestor was meeting his wife on "the astral plane" and then he explained that each of us has a second self that comes and goes from our physical bodies all the time. Some of us are aware of this, but most of us aren't.

Then Everett had an announcement. He announced that Jo-Jo moved into the comic shop because it was the best thing for her to do because her parents were making it hard for her to go on living at home. He made up a cot for her in a little room in the back. But that wasn't the best thing. The best thing was that he and Jo-Jo are engaged. They plan to get married after the baby is born. Everett has a name picked out: Virgil. Jo-Jo likes it, but if it turns out to be a girl, she wants to call it Virginia, which they both like too.

They even went to a tattoo shop and each had a little 'v' put on their shoulders. Everett has his 'v' on his left shoulder, and Jo-Jo has her 'v' on her right shoulder.

Everyone applauded, and gathered around Everett and Jo-Jo congratulating them.

They all went out to a restaurant after our meeting, but I decided to get back to Eva's house and relieve Myron so he could have something left of his evening.

Later, after Myron left, and Roxy was tucked in, and Eva took some pain pills I had given her, so she was sleeping, I tried to write the report on the conference. It's a requirement. Every time you do something where there's money spent on you doing it, you have to explain why. Then you have to give details about what you learned and how it will help you in your job.

I started in on the paperwork, and got to the part about giving a summary of the trip, and set it aside. It was just too much.

Instead, I thought I'd write to Dana. We've been exchanging a few emails since I left Philadelphia, mostly about professional stuff like new exhibits, digitizing materials, and things like that. I did include a personal experience: I told her a little about Roxy, mainly how she's my niece and that we do things together, but not about Eva.

Dana wrote about a trip she took to New York City to monitor a display of loaned historical materials from her library to the big New

York one. The items were irreplaceable, and therefore, extremely valuable. Dana went along to make sure they were properly cared for, and returned in the same condition they were before they went out on loan.

I was writing Dana about some things I thought she'd be interested in, like my book collecting, and while I was writing, I kept nodding off, then pulling myself together for another sentence only to doze off again. I finally gave up and went to bed.

I ARRIVED A FEW MINUTES EARLY the next morning, so I thought I'd finish up the letter to Dana I began last night. No sooner had I started, I stopped.

Mr. Bynes was standing next to me. He had a child's sweater in his hand. It was thin and pink.

"I found this in the children's section. One of the girls must have forgotten to take it with her."

"Why don't you turn it in to Ms. Wills?" I asked. "She takes care of any lost or misplaced items." I didn't tell him why—because Ms. Wills has to keep track of everything.

"It might not look right," and held it out to me. "You take it."

I pretended not to know what he meant.

"You see," he said, "I know—I've known for some time—that people have been watching me."

"No," I said, "that's not true."

"But it is. I've been noticing it more and more. I don't feel comfortable. I haven't felt comfortable for a long time."

He was still holding the sweater out to me.

"You should return it to Ms. Wills yourself," I repeated.

"It would be awkward."

Then he told me there were times when he'd be working and he sensed the presence of someone close by. When he turned around, there would be Ms. Wills, staring at him. If their eyes met, she'd smile, then pretend she was doing some busy work.

He looked determined. "If I gave her this," he looked at the sweater, "she will ask all kinds of questions. I know she will. I don't want to be embarrassed, not again, not ever."

It was difficult for me to say anything, but still, I asked, "Why?" as if I didn't know about him, or his past, and thinking if I acted naïve, he might believe I didn't know anything about him. That was a mistake.

"You know why," he said.

I took the sweater from his hand, and laid it on my desk.

He started to leave, then turned back.

"I wasn't honest the other night when I told the group about my worst experience."

"You weren't?"

"No. It wasn't about the day when I was abandoned as a boy. It was the day I was convicted, when I realized my conviction was real, and how serious it was."

"I don't know if I should be hearing about this," I said.

"It's all right. I should have been truthful before now, but I wasn't. Besides, it really doesn't matter at this point. I've already made my decision. I won't be around here anymore. I can't stay. But you should know that what I've done is not what people say I've done, or anything like what you may have heard." Then he told me about how he was convicted.

He had been working for a security company full-time for a couple of years in Pittsburg, and the company had a contract from one of the school boards to erect a fence around some vacant property the board purchased to increase the size of the playground so it would meet state guidelines. There's supposed to be so much ground for so many kids. There's even an equation for it.

"It was getting late in the afternoon," he said, "maybe 4:30, one of those fall days when the sun starts going down, and there wasn't much time left before dark, maybe an hour or so, and we just finished putting up a section of chain link.

I noticed this kid sitting across the lot. It was a sand lot, nothing on it. Anyway, he was just sitting there. He must have been watching us since the end of the school day.

We were putting our tools away in the truck and he comes over. He wants to know what we're doing. Instead of trying to explain, I ask him where's his mom. She's supposed to pick him up, but she hasn't, and the kid doesn't know where she is.

My partner wants to get on the road, get through traffic, and home before dark. Technically, for us the day is over. I say, 'Go ahead. Take the truck.'

My apartment wasn't that far away, and I figured I could walk. I couldn't leave the kid alone in the empty lot especially when right across the street is one of those gas stations which is also a food and beverage stop. It has a couple of tables where you can sit and watch the street out the window. I thought we could get a soda, and wait there for his mom to show up.

He says that's what he wants to do, too. Yeah, I mean we could see everything from the big window, you know? He'd point out his mom's car when it drove up, then I'd take him back across the street so he'd be safe through the traffic. It was the least I could do.

We have sodas. We wait. Mom doesn't come. The kid gets anxious, looks like he might break down and cry. Really misses his mom. I hold him, and tell him everything will be all right.

The cashier sees this. I didn't know it at the time. The cashier didn't know anything about this kid, or about me, or that he was stranded, or what he was going through, or the fact that I was actually looking out for him. Yeah, well, that was just one person who testified later. Another one was an employee in PetSmart.

PetSmart was right next door. I thought I'd take the kid to see the strays, the cats and dogs they have from the shelter. They're all in cages waiting to be adopted.

He just wants something to hold. It's getting dark. Even the pets can't keep him from fretting.

I rub his hair and take him by the shoulders and tell him everything will be all right. Just about that time, mom shows up. She's frantic.

Doesn't let me explain anything. Half the time she's yelling at her kid, and the other half she's shaking her finger at me.

The next thing I know, I'm in cuffs."

"Surely, reason prevailed," I said.

"Reason? Nope. I was held without bail. They got the kid to say all kinds of stuff. I mean, you can get kids to say anything, especially if they're all worked up, like this kid.

At the trial I finally realized that everybody wanted me locked up. It was frightening."

"And you were only trying to do a good deed?"

"Exactly. But nobody saw it that way. I guess mainly because they thought I was a repeat offender."

"Have you had this kind of thing happen before?" I asked.

"Not really. Well . . . there was the time I took off an afternoon and went to the zoo. There was a kid that was left behind. I mean, this little guy was lost. By the time I took him over to the park's office, I was being accused of all kinds of things."

The next day, Mr. Bynes didn't report for work. He left without resigning, or leaving a message, or a farewell, or anything at all. He just went off. I don't know if we will ever hear from him.

I HAD TIME TO STOP by the hospice to see Eva. Roxy was at softball practice—she's a catcher for the team now—and I could pick her up later in the evening.

"Your sister, Eva, she's out of it," the nurse said.

"Out of it?" I asked.

"Yes. She's incoherent, and she can't help herself anymore."

Eva's like Mama. She's too weak to push the plunger for the morphine drip.

It's hard to see her this way. She's pale as a ghost, and so skinny her bones show. Her face is hollow, and her eyes are closed, and her mouth is open like she's trying to breathe but her breathing is so slight, it's difficult to know if she's breathing or not. Sometimes I put my cheek by her mouth to see if I can feel her breath.

Every time I visit, I talk to the nurse. She knows how concerned I am, and how difficult it is to watch my sister experience the same things as Mama did before she died.

I was sitting at Mama's beside, and the nurse—I call her the good nurse—came over and placed her palm—it was cool—on the side of my face and gently pressed it against her hip. I could smell the starch from her uniform.

"It won't be long now," she said, trying to console me. "Why don't you go home? Get some sleep. I'll take care of your sister. She should rest easier tonight, and you can see her tomorrow."

When I visited the hospice center the next day, I learned that Eva had become one of the unfortunates.

It was clear that I had to make arrangements, something I didn't want to face, and I had been putting off, but as it turned out, I didn't have to worry about it at all.

When I called the funeral home, the one we used for Mama, the funeral director said, "Everything has been taken care of."

I had no idea of what he meant.

"Usually the family arranges for services and burial. In this case," he broke off, "well, let me ask you, did your sister discuss any of this with you beforehand?"

It was then I remembered the envelope.

Soon as I was off the 'phone, I went to the nightstand, opened the drawer and there it was right on top. Inside, there was only one page, and it was folded over. It had one sentence. It was in Eva's handwriting. It said, "Please see Mr. Turner," and gave a telephone number.

When I called, an operator answered and said, "You've reached the law offices of DUCETTE, WAITTS, RAHN AND TURNER. How may I help you?"

"Eva, my sister—you may know her—asked me to call."

"You must be Ms. Stryk then. Our condolences on your loss. Mr. Turner has been expecting your call, and would like to meet with you. I can arrange an appointment at your convenience."

I'm supposed to drive over tomorrow. It's in a part of town I normally don't go to, not for any special reason; they're just businesses and professional offices, and I've never needed any of the services there. When I spoke with Myron, he offered to go with me if I wanted. I thought the company would be nice, so I agreed.

That night, I had my talk with Roxy. She was more understanding than I expected.

"We didn't want her to be sick anymore, did we?" she asked.

"That's right."

"Well, now she's not sick, is she?"

"No," I said.

Roxy cried, but I don't think it's really settled in yet. I expect she will experience more grief in the coming weeks, maybe months, as she comes to fully understand her loss.

Later, when she was wiping her tears away, I promised her that we could go camping.

The next day, when Myron came over to pick me up to go to the law offices, he brought a plant with him. "It's not much,' he said, "just a reminder of another living thing."

It's a spider plant.

Myron is convinced it produces extra oxygen, and thought I might want to put it in my garage to improve the air quality, but I've not been there lately, staying at my sister's house and all.

Before we left to see the attorney, Myron kissed me. He met me at the door, then half-way down the steps, he stopped. I did too. He took my head in his hands, and bent down and touched his lips to my hairline. So I guess it was a forehead kiss.

I drove the truck. Myron knew where the office was located.

As we came closer to the attorney's office I had an increasing sense of apprehension, like a giant hand closing itself around me.

We were shown to a conference office with big padded chairs around a modern, polished wood table.

While we were waiting for Mr. Turner, Myron said, "The lawyers don't let you know where their real offices are—probably hidden somewhere in the back of the building—because the people they help may go back there and find them and hurt them. Sometimes, they tell their secretaries to say they are in, when they are out, and at other times, out, when they are in. They do this so they can avoid facing their clients, when they have to."

We were offered tea or coffee while we waited. Myron went for the green tea; I didn't want anything. I felt nauseous. It came in waves.

Mr. Turner came into the conference room talking, "There's no question about my intention to attend your sister's funeral, but that turned out to be impossible. Something urgent came up. Please accept my sincere apologies."

He brought a folder with him, and soon as he sat down, he opened it up. It was thick with lots of legal papers. It was all about Eva and her stuff.

"Ummmm. This *is* a personal matter. Perhaps your companion might be more comfortable in the waiting area?"

I said, "This is Myron. I want Myron to be here, and Myron wants to be here."

Mr. Turner looked at us both blankly—no expression at all. "All right then, let's get on with it."

Before he could get on with it, I said, "Eva didn't like wood much."

"Wood?" Mr. Turner asked.

"Yes. You put her in a plain wood casket."

"That was your sister's wish—to keep the costs down."

"She never said anything about that."

"Yes, she did." He held up a piece of paper. "It's right here. I took notes whenever she came in."

"When Mama died, Eva and I took care of her funeral arrangements. I always thought taking care of things like this was a matter for family."

"Usually that is the case. As for me, I'm afraid my involvement comes with the job," he smiled. "One of those things you do for your clients. See, Ms. Stryk, your sister, for many years, worked closely with our staff here in accounting. During the course of that time, she became a respected member of our team, so to speak, and therefore it was natural for her to turn to us for her legal work, mainly her trust."

"Trust?"

"Yes. It was necessary. Eva's estate was substantial. You may have guessed as much. In fact, we're still processing her financial assets. Those figures should be available in three or four weeks, I suspect. As your sister's trustee, it is my obligation to explain the conditions of her trust to you. Also, it might please you to know you are a distributee."

"I don't understand," I said, "why I didn't know about any of this?"

Myron took my hand for a moment. "A trust requires at least one witness, Mr. Turner," Myron said. "Who was the witness?"

He flipped through some pages, "Ah, here it is, the witness was Mr. Waitts, an honorable person, I assure you."

"Mr. Waitts? Is he a member of your firm?" Myron asked.

"Why yes. This is done frequently. We want an objective third party, you know," Mr. Turner said, and then produced a long document in blue paper wrappers. "Eva left you temporal care of the house in which you may live until Roxanne reaches age of majority, or 21 years. At that time, she becomes sole owner.

You will have an allowance, however, to care for your niece, monitored through this office."

"Do you mean Frances has to ask permission to provide from the estate for her niece?" Myron asked.

"Yes. Well, there's a monthly maintenance sum—we'll discuss the amount later—and for items that are more expensive, Ms. Stryk will have to provide paperwork, that's all. We can get into details later."

"What about her things?" I asked.

"*Things*? What do you mean," Mr. Turner asked.

"Her personal things. There are items we inherited from our parents. Eva had my mother's engagement diamond, all her brooches, my father's wedding ring, his coin collection—"

"We've already been to the safety deposit box—this is routine by the way—and there wasn't much there of any material value, no rings, coins, other jewelry, and so forth. There was the property title, which we're working with at the moment. The remainder of the estate, stocks, bonds, cash, any investment instruments, have been placed in a special account."

Mr. Turner shrugged. "Your sister was very clear in her wishes. If matters like these are not discussed with other family members, we don't pry. Eva never explained why she chose this particular distribution of her assets. Even if she had confided in us—which I assure you she did not—we could not disclose anything relative to those conversations. You understand."

Myron spoke up. "As sole trustee, can you give an estimate of what you may expect to acquire from the estate?"

"I wish I could, but at this time, it would be impossible to estimate." He paused, and looked up at the ceiling like he was trying to imagine something.

"Considering how old Roxanne is now, it will be about a decade before she reaches age of majority, so that means monitoring the estate during that period, and I couldn't possibly determine the fees involved at this time. A trustee's sum for time in research, and distribution is limited by the state. What? Around five percent? I can't recall just now . . ." His voice trailed off as he shuffled through the papers.

"What was the cost of the trust itself? Surely you must have that figure," Myron asked.

Mr. Turner worked himself through more papers. When he found the original trust, he held it up. "Eva's estate required considerable conversion. Ah, here it is, and I should add, consistent with sums charged for similar estate work. It's standard."

"What would be standard?" Myron asked.

"About . . . mmmm . . . about suh, suh, sixty."

"Sixty?" Myron asked. "Sixty what?"

"Sixty thousand."

Mr. Turner then glanced at Myron, then glanced back to me, then again to Myron. "Trusts require significant work, and I'm not saying they can't be broken, but for all practical purposes, they are unassailable. I've seen attorneys, even a probate judge or two, do anything rather than challenge a trust by trial."

"Would you say trusts are stock-in-trade then?" Myron asked.

"Certainly. We create trusts, as do other estate attorneys, on a continuing basis."

Mr. Turner reached in his suit coat pocket, withdrew a silver case with a stylized 'T' in a circle in the center, clicked it open and removed two business cards. He held them out, one in each hand, for Myron and me.

"If you should ever wish to establish a trust, please let me know. I'd be happy to help you secure your financial futures."

He turned away from the table, pushed his roller chair over to the door, opened it and, holding the trust and other papers, asked his secretary to make copies for me.

When we got outside, I asked Myron if he'd drive the truck, take us back home.

LATER BEFORE GOING to bed, I thought I'd check my email. When I opened my inbox, I saw a message from Dana. It was short. She wanted to know if there was a time she could call.

At first, I thought she wanted to talk to me about Eva, to tell me she's sorry for my loss, maybe because everyone else is doing that now, the way people do, but how could Dana know about Eva, especially since I never mentioned Eva to her? It had to be something else then. I don't know what I was thinking. I wrote back and said she could call "any time."

I wasn't up very long the next morning, still making breakfast for Roxy in the kitchen when the 'phone rang.

Dana began by saying her library in Philadelphia anticipates the retirement of a senior librarian in rare books and manuscripts in about a year. It's already been announced, which meant Dana wasn't doing anything unprofessional by telling me. She said, "Maybe you would consider applying when the library begins taking applications. If you like the idea, I would be willing to bring your résumé to the attention of the hiring committee."

Dana made it clear that I wouldn't be applying for the senior librarian's position. That would be filled internally by another person already on the staff with years and years of service. That person's job would be filled by another in-house librarian, and so on down the line, eventually creating an entry-level vacancy.

"It's a nice thought, it really is," I said because I wanted Dana to know how much I appreciated her calling like that, "but the fact is, I'm not qualified, not even for an entry-level position in special collections."

She explained that all I needed was certification in archives and rare books, and that's about 12 graduate credits. I could take some hybrid online classes which would mean I'd drive into the city maybe twice a semester.

"If you put your mind to it, you could be certified in a year, or about the time the position will become vacant."

Dana went on, "I can't promise anything, you understand, although if you did receive your certification, it's likely you would get an interview."

If it's anything I know, it's librarians. If Dana alerts the selection committee they would ask—it always happens—if Dana knows the applicant, informally of course, and if in her opinion, the candidate would fit in, meaning can she work with their team, given all their different personalities, and so on. Before you know it, they're all discussing the applicant, and that can be a good thing, though I've seen it backfire.

The following week, I spoke to Ms. Wills about taking a few classes. I didn't tell her anything about why, other than some reference to "personal enrichment," and also, I would need someone to look after the writers' circle.

"Do you have anyone in mind?" she asked.

"I hadn't thought about it," I said, but I had. I thought Myron would be perfect.

Ms. Wills seemed like she would consider the idea, that she was open.

The college gives special consideration to faculty for public service. It's called outreach. Myron's always doing outreach anyway. He gives talks to the Rotary, the Kiwanis, and other organizations in town, so it'd be a natural for him.


I WANTED TO GET ROXY'S MIND off Eva, so we went downtown to the outdoors sports store and bought a tent. Roxy picked it out. It has a double canopy, and a sewn-in, moisture-resistant floor. It's the best. Roxy and I agree. Then she wanted a pair of hiking boots just like mine.

We camp out whenever we get the chance. We take the truck and fill up the flat bed and go to the best hiking trails and campsites in northwestern Pennsylvania.

I told Roxy that by the end of the year, when I get my certificate in special collections, and if I get that interview in Philadelphia, she can go with me and we could hike the Wissahickon.

# THE CHILDREN'S PRISON

LEGISLATORS SAY our state is the first to have anything like it. It's their way of fixing the justice system so it can respond to the increasing number of juvenile criminals. The warden says that it's a development of modern penology and soon our model will be adopted throughout the nation.

It's called Annex A—that's the official name—and it took two years to create. Our medium security prison at Albion was chosen as the site, and the buildings were put up in a cluster. Pods. Multi-colored. Each pod has five kids. Some of the local merchants donated playground equipment, but it isn't used much. Even though it may appear to be a more sensitive and caring environment, it's still a prison.

The facility planners tried to keep the concertina wire and chain link and cement pads to a minimum. It's all still here, just covered by plants and trees, and the concrete has a rubber coating so it's softer to walk on, and if a kid falls down playing, it's not so bad. The video system and lockdown security is state of the art.

They may be kids, but they're all here for the same reason. They may have committed the worst crimes, yet people can't get over the fact they are still kids. So they don't get the death penalty. It's life without parole, and as long as they're here, they're separated from the main prison population. Some of these kids have no idea what they've done. If they do, they don't act like it.

About six months before Annex A was completed, the warden let guards apply for the children's prison. Those who wanted to work here were screened, given an interview by a board which included Warden Coop, Dr. Woo, an Albion family psychiatrist, and a couple from town who ran a foster home for years. They never had kids of their own and when they retired everybody thought it would be a natural to have a mom-and-pop team on site, available for the residents.

The guards who were chosen were given six months of special training, courses in abnormal child psychology, criminal behaviors of minors, care of the incarcerated, and courses in human growth and motivation.

That's the first thing you learn when you become a juvenile guard: you think you can rehabilitate them. It's only natural; we want to believe these behaviors can be changed, especially with a younger population. They seem just like other kids; they have a sense of wonder, a natural inquiry, open to new ideas, so you fall for it. But they're all typed. That's what you learn. They all have a biotype. It's right there on the first page of their file. There are days when you think some of these kids can do anything. And you can never get too close to any of them. We hear that all the time.

Each guard is assigned five residents. I make sure my five get to Group which meets three times a week, recreation, chow hall, and in between those activities, they're all doing what they're supposed to be doing. They have their assignments to work on from Group, tasks like writing, artwork, and reading. My job is to keep them on track.

The assignments usually have something to do with self-discovery, so they can find out who they are. And goals. Goals are a big thing around here. The idea is that they have something to work towards to improve themselves. It'd be great if it worked out that way.

Every resident has their own room in the pod. We call it a room, but it's really a cell, it's just camouflaged with designs. Each kid picks a theme. It can be cartoon character, fantasy murals, rock stars, athletes, like that.

Each cell has its own security window with a special shade, it's accordion steel and operates electronically. All the resident has to do is push a button. If the kid in the next cell wants to see and talk, there's a vented grate at the base of the window. When the shade goes up, the other inmate hears the motor pulling up the metal plate, and can do the same, or leave his side down. Sometimes one kid wants to talk, and the other one doesn't. We get quite a few requests to exchange cells based on who wants to 'visit' his neighbor, and who doesn't. In other words, who likes who. And if you know anything about kids, you know they change their minds all the time.

Each resident has a play corner in their cell—until they're 12. They can put anything they want in the play corner. They can paint it, keep toys there, and it's considered a special place. You can find all kinds of creations there: doll houses, primitive murals, drawings of family members, even graffiti. On the resident's 13th birthday, the play corner is no longer permitted.

Each cell has a single 'view window' which faces the play area so the child can see trees and grass, and when the recreation periods begin, they can see other kids out there as well. And they know they will be out there too, every day for at least one hour. Gives them something to look forward to when they're not busy.

They can use the playground through their 12th year, then it's prohibited. At that time they are transferred to "The Green" which is really a replacement for the old "Yard." It's for all the kids between 13 and 18. They can play handball there, or climb the rocks, which is very popular. Kids love heights, so the warden put in some stone pylons with metal grips so they can climb up on them and jump off. They'll play dodgeball off of them too. But all this changes when they turn 18.

Every kid has a prison name. Can't be helped. The first kid on my block is Alan Rodriguez, but he's called Pogo. Everyone calls him that. He likes it. He has more energy than any kid in here. Even guards have names.


## POGO


I'll be out of here in a few months, transferred to another facility. The guard reminds me every day. His name is Señor Blanco, that's what I call him. He tells me I'm going to the big lock up for adults. It's where we all go when we turn 18, but I have a plan.

I've been here for three years. Most of the kids have trouble admitting what they've done, but not me. I know and I'm all right with it. It needed to be done. I was the first one in our Group to explain myself. This is what I told them.

When I was 14 I fell in love. Her name was Marianne, and she was beautiful. Her real dad died when she was little, and her step-dad was a dick, so her mom had to work while the step-dad stayed home and complained about everything. I remember the night it happened just like a movie that keeps playing in my head.

We're going out for the evening, so I go over to pick her up. Sometimes we'd just go downtown and walk around, or sit in the park. Talk about things. I get to the door and her little brother is there and says she's crying in her room. "All messed up," is what he says.

He tells me Anthony—that's their step-dad—told Marianne she couldn't go out because no one was home but him and he didn't want to be home by himself. It was a real thing with him maybe because he wanted somebody to wait on him and boss around. He'd been drinking too. They got into a fight in the kitchen and Anthony picks up the frying pan which is right off the burner, and he waves it at her. Marianne doesn't shut up. She keeps arguing with him and that's when he pushes the pan in her face.

There's a big mark by the side of her mouth where the skin's burned away. Her little brother wants her to go to the hospital, but she refuses. Marianne tells herself that is she thinks it's not so bad, maybe it won't be. She runs off to her bedroom, and Anthony's sleeping it off on the couch in the living room.

I go to her bedroom door and talk softly to her. She doesn't want anything to do with anybody. I wait awhile, then I go home.

It's a couple of weeks before I see her again. She has a scar—it's slick and wine-colored—by the side of her mouth, like half a clown mouth, like the Joker in Batman. It's rounded a little, looks like the edge of a frying pan. Anthony says it's a reminder to her about talking too much.

We meet on the porch in the morning while Anthony is still asleep. I'm careful about what I say. But I know she needs something medical, a skin graft or something.

She doesn't want to talk about it. I say, "Marianne, you have to talk sometime. You have to talk to *somebody*."

She goes inside. Her brother says she just "mopes around." This goes on for weeks, then the next thing I know, she's gone. Nobody can find her. Her mom calls the police and they put out a bulletin for a couple of days, then there's a search. They look everywhere. The cops talk to her step-dad, her mom, her brother, me. Then there's the discovery.

There's a train tunnel outside of town. It goes through one of the mountains. Must be a mile long. That's where they found her. No one could identify her. They had to go by dental records. The coroner said it might have been an accident, but probably not. He couldn't find alcohol or drugs in her blood, and that's when I started to think up my plan.

The old man—the step-dad—when he's sober and feels like doing something, works on junk cars. He's got one of them in his backyard. It's all torn down, and he's trying to fix it up.

So I start hanging around the house. At first he doesn't take to this, but whenever I go over, I take a six pack. I stay for an hour or so, then come back a few days later. Same thing. We talk cars. He gives me advice. I take it, you know.

This goes on for about a month. One day I drive over and tell him I got a buddy who wants to get rid of a '48 Dodge just like the one in his back yard. Maybe it'd be good for parts, I tell him, then I offer to drive him over and take a look at the car. I even have a cold six pack on front seat.

But instead of going over to see the car I made up, we drive straight through town. He wants to know where we're goin' and all I say is just hold on, and I drive off the road near the train tunnel onto a gravel area below the grade so the car can't be seen from the highway.

He wants to know what's goin' on, and when I just stare at him, he swings open the door, and is about to hustle out, when I take out my dad's .45 I have under the seat and put it under his chin and tell him to put his hands on the dash.

That's when I cuff him and push him out of the car. I get a burlap bag out of the back seat with my stuff and we're off.

I tell him to walk in front of me and I keep the .45 at the back of his head. We walk right into the tunnel and we keep on walking until I say stop.

When I figure we are about halfway through the tunnel, I tell him to sit down. Soon as I do this, he starts to cry. I take out my trowel from the bag and start digging around one of the rail ties. Soon as I dig deep enough, I take out the chain from the bag and one of those super strength locks you get at the hardware store.

I wind the chain through the cuffs, pull him down as close to the rails as I can, and snap the lock shut. I tell him, "You're not going to get out of this one." Then he pleads with me and says all kinds of things: he's sorry, he didn't know what he was doing, he never thought Marianne would hurt herself, and like that.

After he talked himself out, I got my burlap bag and my trowel. I told him, "I don't know when the next train's coming in here, but it'll be enough time for you to think about what you did to Marianne."

I woulda' got away with it too, just like it shoulda' been, but it was the cuffs. I got them from a high school buddy who worked in a government surplus store in town. They're always getting contraband stuff and that's where I got the cuffs. Even though they'd seen a lot of use and were mangled up pretty bad, the cops traced them to the store, and they told my buddy to be honest with them, or he'd be an accessory, so he 'fessed up.

When I told my story in Group, Dr. Woo—his prison name is Voodoo, and that's what we call him, but we can't call him that in Group—nodded and said, "You are beginning a new journey to a new self because you kept to the facts of your case. Honesty is the first step in understanding ourselves. Alan—" he said, using my file name, "the other members would benefit by being as open as you have been with us. Thank you."

Dr. Woo asked Mom and Pop if this wasn't so, and Mom and Pop agreed. Pop said, "We are all here to heal ourselves and face what is troubling us so we can become better human beings."

Voodoo asked if there were other volunteers who'd want to tell their story. No one answered and it was quiet for a long time, then Voodoo asked Jam-Jam to tell her story, but she refused.

Jam-Jam is in a neighbor cell, and she's having a hard time because everything is new to her. She's only been in Annex A for a few weeks.

"It's all right," I say. "You can talk here, you know? Everybody understands. We're all here for the same reason."

But she shakes her head "no" like before and hugs her stuffed toy which she drags around with her everywhere, even though she's 13.

Mom takes a special interest in her, probably because she's so young. "Kim," she say, (that's her other name, the one that doesn't work anymore, Kimberly Lovehorn,) "maybe you'd like to talk to me another time? We could have a little visit, just you and me. What do you think about that?"

Jam-Jam looks at her like she's going to cry. But then she stiffens up. Her eyes get narrow and her mouth is tight.

Mom sees this and backs off, but not Voodoo. He tries to get her to open up. He promises extra playground time, but it doesn't work. Next he tries a double serving of her favorite dessert. No go.

I'm kind of like an older brother to her. I don't say anything when she talks to me. She already told me about her crime, but she never calls it a crime. She calls it "the mistake." She'll say, "The mistake put me here."

I offered her one of my pictures. I draw pictures of territories I want. Voodoo asked me to do this once and I've been doing it ever since. Like I should have patience, so I draw a place where patience would be. Then it's mine. A country I call Patience. It has palm trees and beaches and everything is calm there. Dr. Voodoo says this way I can improve myself. I have drawings of all kinds of countries: Hope, Certainty, High Times, and like that.

I offered Jam-Jam one of my drawings if she told me about her crime. I gave her "Tunnel Life," about a country that is connected by all kinds of tunnels like twisted up garden hoses. Each tunnel has a name. I started with the alphabet—'A' for Alpha, and like that.

"I'll tell you then," she agreed one afternoon when we were talking through the grate, "but you can't say anything to anybody. For true?"

"For true," I swore.

"Not even to Mr. Harry Bones," she said. That's what Jam-Jam calls Señor Blanco.

"Not even him," I said.

"Ok, you promise," and then she told me about the "mistake."

Jam-Jam and her sister needed money for Xtacy and they knew about a convenience store in the neighborhood. The night clerk was a local guy—everybody knows him—and he was mousy so they figured he was a push over. All they had to do was threaten him and he'd turn over the cash pronto.

They hung around outside until the place looked empty, and when it looked like nobody was coming in, they put scarves on, like bandits, you know? And hit 'em up. Jam-Jam's sis put her hand in her pocket like she had a gun, and soon as she started talking, telling him to hand over the cash in the register, or she'd blow him away, he looked real curious.

He opened the register, stopped, walked around the counter with his head cocked to one side then he started to smile even though he was being threatened.

"Wai—t just a minute here. You guys are the Lovehorn sisters, aren't cha'? Sure, I can tell." Then he began laughing and made a move toward Jam-Jam's sister to remove her scarf. That's when Jam-Jam jumped over the counter, grabbed the money from the register, and the clerk lunged for her sister. When Jam-Jam saw the clerk wrestling with her sister, she looked around for something to stop him, and the only thing behind the counter was a baseball bat.

By this time, her sister and the cashier were down on the floor struggling. Jam-Jam lifted the bat high, waiting until she could take a good shot at his head, but just at the moment she brought it down, he moved, and the bat cracked her sister's skull.

Soon as she saw what she had done, she ran out of the store. The night clerk called 911 but her sister was dead before they could get her to a hospital. Jam-Jam was picked up later that night. She had fallen to sleep in the back of her parents' car with her stuffed toy.

Some of us wonder about her. It doesn't look like she's fitting in here. I mean she's not making many friends and that's really important in Annex A.

## SEÑOR BLANCO, MR. HARRY BONES,
## A.K.A. RUSSELL NEWHOUSE

Kids. Who can figure? You have to do something for them. Dr. Woo invited me to a couple of sessions, with the permission of Mom and Pop, and of course, the other residents. The idea was this: if guards learn more about the residents, then maybe they can help them more. It's understanding why they behave like they do.

We're trying to work with Pogo who's been giving tattoos to the other residents. The warden thinks we should put a stop to that. What might be good for one kid, might not be good for another. And Jam-Jam will get a play corner for one year even though she's over 12 because she's new and it might help her adjust. So far, all she's done is sit in her corner with her stuffed toy, but I suspect she will come around—sometime. We are optimistic here. It's part of our pledge. It's important to be.

NYLON might be considered a model for Group. He's overcoming his fears which put him here in the first place. The facts in his case are pretty clear: he always played with younger kids even though his parents discouraged him.

He was building a snow igloo, rolling the balls then packing them down when one of the children who lived near his house—the families knew each other—came over to play. She was eight, and Nylon, whose outside name that doesn't mean anything now that he's here, was Vernon Wright, Jr., and he was a few years older than the new girl who wanted to play igloo.

They worked together on the snow house and what happened next was just a child's reaction. If you think about it, you wonder if it was a crime at all. I mean, it could happen to anyone.

The girl, who by all accounts was a darling child, found an iron bar in the yard. Workmen must have left it when they completed a cement patio earlier that year. It's used to reinforce concrete. She brought it to Nylon thinking he would like it. Maybe they could use it somehow. But Nylon was busy packing snow. She handed it to him, then stepped back. He examined it, finally deciding it was of no use, and threw it behind him.

The rod slipped easily out of his mitten, which was icy, so it flew with some force. It rotated in the air and stuck the little girl. Nylon didn't even realize she was unconscious until several minutes later when he called her name and she didn't answer. Once he saw the blood on the snow, he panicked.

Nylon tried to revive her, but he couldn't. Instead, he piled up the snow, went to his house, found a tarp and waited for evening. Just before dark, he went out, bundled her in the tarp and carried her up the back stairs of his home to his room. He put her under the bed hoping she would wake up and everything would be all right again.

It was a question for the court whether she ever became conscious, but apparently when she began to moan, Nylon panicked, fearing his parents would hear and he would be in more trouble than ever, so he just wanted her noise to go away.

He tried whispering to her, then he shook her, thinking he could bring her around so he could tell her to shut up. There was no stopping her moaning.

He ran down the hall, came to a laundry basket and reached in for the first thing he could find and it was a pair of his mother's panty hose. Within a couple of minutes, he no longer had to be afraid of the sounds she'd been making.

I was there when he gave his account of the crime during Group.


## NYLON


"Because it was an accident, I'm always thinking I might get my sentence commuted," Nylon said.

"Not a chance," Pogo said. "We're all lifers here."

Dr. Woo raised his eyebrows. Mom and Pop had the look of distance, like they were far away someplace, unavailable for comment.

Jam-Jam said, "I had an accident too."

Dr. Woo patted a stack of folders. "An important part of our sessions is self-awareness. Here we learn to deal with the facts. We must know the truth, and then we must learn to live with the truth we know. So there are two things we must do. Each of you has a factual record of your crime. In Vernon's case, there's forensic evidence to give us the facts. Right, Vernon?"

"I suppose."

"You suppose?" asked Dr. Woo. "Exactly what do you suppose?"

"The stuff you said."

"Forensic evidence?"

"Yeah, that's it."

"What do you think that might be, Vernon?"

"Stuff."

"What kind of stuff?"

"I dunno."

"Well, shouldn't we find out?" and Dr. Woo looked around at the other residents like this was a really good idea. Then he opened the file that said, "WRIGHT, JR., VERNON" and took out an official looking document.

"Now this is a post-mortem op report. It tells us what happened. Why don't we let Vernon read it, then he might want to offer some comment. Vernon?" Dr. Woo handed him the sheet.

Vernon took a few minutes. His face lost its color and his skin wrinkled up, "Nah," he said. "There's somthin' wrong here. Boomer—" (that's Nylon's name for me—) "told me I was probably right. It was an accident."

Everybody knew Dr. Woo was uncomfortable with this information. He just looked like it. But like I said, you have to give these kids something.

"Vernon," Dr. Woo began again, "What was the young girl's name?"

"I forget."

"Wel—l, let's see if our file can be of help. Ah, yes, here it is. Her name was Rose. Rose O'Malley. Do you remember Rose?"

"Kinda."

Dr. Woo handed a photograph to Vernon, then after he looked at it, he wanted Vernon to pass it around to everybody. "This is a school picture," Dr. Woo said.

"Now in the file, there's another picture of Rose. It was taken at her autopsy. There's a little diagram that goes with it. It shows how the iron rod lodged in her body. It entered through—"

"Yeah," Nylon interrupted, "she probably fell on it. Those things were sticking up all over. Like I told you, an accident."

Dr. Woo said we all had to work on understanding ourselves and we couldn't expect to know everything in a short time, after all, it took a long time to get us to where we are now. Then he closed the session with The Promise Ring. We all held hands in a circle and made a promise for patience and insight and for knowledge too, so we'd know what to do with the patience and insight.

Later after supper, I went on my rounds for bed check, and I heard Nylon crying.

The next day I brought him some vampire comics which he really likes to read.


CAT


Cat's the pod baby. He's eight. He looks up to me.

He's in because his mom told him to give his baby brother a bath. She said, "It's your job. Go wash him."

Cat did just that. He was cleaning him in the bathinette, and they were both laughing and playing with the water and the rubber toys, when his brother peed on him. He didn't mean to. Mr. Harry Bones says it was an "involuntary response." Says so in the report. But when the baby peed straight up in the air and hit Cat in the face, he pushed him under the water and kept him there. When he finally let him go, he didn't move.

During play period, I push Cat on the swing and talk to him. Dr. Woo says that's a good thing. Mom and Pop are proud of me too. It's kind of like a job. One of my responsibilities. In Group we learn that when we help others we help ourselves, and we all want to help ourselves a lot so someday we can go home.


## RUSSELL NEWHOUSE

In our weekly newsletter, the warden announced the first award for child resident guards in the history of the prison. It will be called "The Annual Best of Annex A Guard Leader Award," and it comes with a plaque and special privileges. No one knows what the special privileges are yet, even though I asked. Jam-Jam told me that she and the other members of the pod are nominating me. That came as a shock. I can hardly believe it. She even showed me the petition. It has everybody's name on it: Pogo, Nylon, Cat, Jam-Jam, and of course, they all signed their prison names because that's who they are, and took it to Dr. Woo for his endorsement.

Dr. Woo had to think about it. He wasn't an inmate, but they told him he could use his prison name, and it wouldn't be like using his other name. Somehow, they convinced him, and he signed the petition. He signed it "Voodoo." Then the residents took it to Mom and Pop because their approval means a lot, and when they signed, they took it to Warden Coop.

These kids can talk you into just about anything if you let them. Sometimes, I think they could talk themselves right out of here if you gave them half a chance. They have to face what they've done. Like I try to tell them, you're not getting out of this one. But we all get along. We have our ups and downs just like family. Everybody has some hobby or interest that just keeps them going somehow. By and large, the people in our state think Annex A helps children, and helps the problem, the reason why we're all in here.

# HIT

I FIRST MET JESUS when I was a shine girl in Albuquerque. There was a couple of other prisoners in the state van, and once they pulled into the truck stop, the guards took turns handcuffing one prisoner at a time to go use the john.

On the way back, one of the guards came over to get his boots done. Jesus was still cuffed to him, but only one hand, and just stood there while I worked. The guard said something to Annie—I shined with Annie—and when he did, Jesus talked to me with his eyes. I knew it was for real then, like a flash, and it was forever too.

He had a pencil stub in his shirt pocket and when the boss man was talking to Annie, he wrote his name and his convict number on the side of the stand, right there in the wood. It's probably still there today.

We never had to say anything. We both knew we were meant for each other from the beginning. That's what I tell people when they ask why I'm following Jesus. I've followed him through two states now—New Mexico and Arizona—and they just took him up to Colorado to finish his sentence.

He served a lot of time before I met him, though. The justice system likes to keep prisoners moving around whenever they can. It costs a heap, but they don't care. A couple of years here, a couple of years there. It's payback for what they did. Moving them around keeps them from family. It makes visiting tough. Besides, the convicts have to make new connections and adjust. The law just wants to mess with them. That's what prison's about, hurting you more than you've been hurt already. When he gets out we're going back to Arizona for the winter. So it's just a few months now and we'll finally be together. And I was doing ok too, until I hit Denver.

SOMEBODY STOLE MY STUFF at the bus depot and that's why everything else happened. That's why I had to take heat from Dancey and why Officer Arlene set me up to do her dirty work for her. I was just following Jesus, that's all. One thing happens—like my stuff gets stolen while I was sleeping in the bus terminal—and because of that one thing, other bad stuff happens.

I took something on the bus ride in, something to make me sleep, and while I was waiting in the terminal, I laid down with my head on my pack, but it was too hard, so I rolled up my jacket for a pillow. I must have been really out, because when I came around, my pack was gone, and my head was still on my jacket.

Boog calls people who steal other people's stuff like that, "stiffs." All I know is everything I had was in that pack, even my kit, so I could always make money. The only money I had was tucked away on me, so at least I could get my ticket, but when I hit Boulder, I was broke.

I had to start pretty much from scratch.

You want to stay away from the big box stores—Wal-Marts, Targets, places like that. Too many cameras and security guards. The best places are locally-owned businesses, so soon as I hit town, I went to the Five Star Military Outlet.

It was like this: I could go to the shelter, or I could get some things I needed and go to one of the parks, or sneak into some shrubs down along the creek. The shelter was out for a zillion reasons: every night you have to check in by seven, and there's worship which you have to go to, and you're supposed to feel grateful, and the more you feel grateful, the happier you'll be. Then, before you know it, they want to get you into a "Transition Program," organize your life, start a job hunt, and finally actually get one.

I've been through shelters before. And if the one in town is like the others, and I'm thinking it has to be, then there's about a hundred goonies down there, gimps, psychos, you name it. I'll take my chances on the street anytime. I know what's there.

I needed to get some gloves, maybe another pair of socks. It was still March with patches of snow on the ground.

There was some guy hanging around outside the surplus store, and I didn't think much about it. There's always somebody hanging around who knows the local buzz, what's going on with the transients, where to get what you need to get you to where you want to go. He was trying to keep himself warm, turning this way, then that, slapping his hands together. When he saw me, he smiled, like he might be getting ready to hit on me, but I looked away.

There was one guy up front at the register, and when I strolled around the aisles, I didn't see anybody but some kid putting stock away—denim overalls, I think. I waited until there was a customer up at the register and the stock boy went into the back room for more stuff, then I found a pair of gloves and stuffed them in my jacket pocket along with a pair of nice wool socks, and one of those silver foil blankets that folds up real small and you just shake it out at night and it'll keep you warm

So I was all set, until I walked outside. First thing I know, that dancey guy grabbed my elbow and spun me around to face him.

"Hey, I know what you did in there."

"Let me go," I said. "You don't know anything."

"Sure I do. I watched you through the window in that mirror," he pointed at one of those circular mirrors they put in corners to watch customers. I use them myself to see what's going on, like when the cashier's busy, or when he's not.

"Let's make this easy. Drop this off for me—" he held out a tiny plastic bag in his hand—"and we'll call it even."

He had a prison tat—I know them anywhere—and he was trying to pass a kite, white power, maybe coke or something. He had the name of somebody who worked at Burger Barn and needed this pronto, but he couldn't deliver it himself because they wouldn't let him in the place. Off limits. I figured this guy had a rep around town and he needed shills—like me.

"No way," I said.

"Fine. Then I'll turn you in," and he slipped the little bag into his jacket pocket. When he started for the door, I could see the guy behind the counter look at him, then at me, and that's when I took off across the street.

I never thought anything would come of it.


IT WAS LATE in the afternoon, getting on towards dark, and that's the first time I saw Boog. He was down by the creek, the part that runs through one of the parks, and he had a butterfly net. There was a boy standing next to him, waiting. Boog must have borrowed the kid's net even tho' there's no butterflies this time of year, and he kept dipping it until he snagged one of the trout the hatchery stocks in the creek for the kids to catch. He held its tail and thumped its head on a rock. Then he snagged another. When he had his two fish, he gave the kid his net back. The kid put it over his head, and he got excited like something great happened.

Boog was rough, but he had a tarp. It was a little lean-to up on a slope by some trees. I had one myself that I packed with me, before it was stolen. It was Boog's tarp, or curling up in the bushes. It was only one night. I'd get something going in the morning; maybe find some plastic sheeting in a dumpster, something I could string up myself. Besides, this is a college town. Students are always throwing out stuff that other people can use. They don't know better.

I offered to trade my gloves if I could stay under his tarp for the night. But only the part that was away from Boog.

He agreed, and said I could keep the gloves. He gutted the fish right there and let the insides slip into the stream. He cut a couple of switches and pushed them through the trout and it wasn't long before we had a fire going right outside the tarp. He had a bottle of vodka. Let me crack it open too.

At night when it got cold and the fire died out, and we were into the bottle pretty deep, he said we should snuggle up for body heat. We used my foil blanket, but it didn't cover us as much as I wanted it to.

I was drifting off then—and I knew this was coming—he pressed against me like that—and promised me I'd like it.

The wind picked up, one of those icy ones. I didn't want to leave the tarp.

"This won't be special, right?"

"It's always special."

"You know what I mean. I don't want you to get all dopey on me and expect it all the time and follow me around."

I picked up the bottle, but it was empty. I guess we finished it off.

Boog wanted back-door stuff, he even joked about it, "Ruff, ruff," he said like he was a dog or something. He said he'd go easy, and he'd reach around and do my clit at the same time, and how great that'd be. He didn't even want to know how old I was.

I was going to ask him if he was clean, but he was already inside me. It wasn't so bad. He was going at it and at it, his balls slapping my butt, and before long I could feel contractions coming on and as soon as that happened he melted.

After, just to make sure he wasn't going goofy on me, I said, "I'm only here for a few months until Jesus gets out." Then I told him about Jesus, how he got 10 and a half for manslaughter.

But Boog was already asleep.


I FOUND SOME CARDBOARD the next morning in a trash can in the park, and I was tearing it into pieces to put in my boots, when Boog came around.

He tugged at my sweater. My mom gave me the sweater, but that was a long time ago.

"You don't have to wear that," he said.

"What do you mean? I like it."

"Yeah, but it's seen better days. Looks like a rat chewed it."

"You mean those little holes? The moths made 'em. I still like it tho'. It's a good sweater. Warm."

"There's lots of clothes in the Good Will pod in the parking lot over at Safeway's. Just go over and pick out what you want. People drive up and dump their stuff; some real finds. I got this there," he pointed to his knit stocking cap. It was kind of scroungey, but he was proud of it. It was camo, like hunters wear.

He just gave me the reason I needed to get going, and out of there. I said I had some errands to run, then I'd go over to the parking lot and look through the clothes. Boulder's a rich place. There's lots of money, and you wouldn't believe some of the things they throw out—bicycles, appliances, T.V.s that still work, and the restaurants throw out food that's still good. Sometimes they don't wait for the charities to pick it up, so if you time it right, it can work out.

On my way downtown I saw some people coming out of the library. They were eating pastry from a paper bag. The library sells food. There's a skyway across the creek and it connects the two parts of the library. They put art up there—paintings by the locals and prints from famous painters, so it's artsy, a place to take a break, I guess. People sit up there and have a late breakfast, or lunch. They sell coffee and fancy pastry. Yeah, and there's a view of the creek down below.

I noticed the girl behind the counter. She ran the concession. I passed by a couple of times, then stopped. "Hey," I said, "you a college girl?"

She looked away.

I stared at her. I kept staring. Finally, she looked at me and seemed annoyed. "Can I help you?" she asked, but it wasn't nice like it's supposed to be.

"Sure," I said. "There's lots of good things that get tossed, you know? Maybe you could let me back there to browse around for a minute. Just turn your back, ok?"

In a corner behind the counter there was a big gray plastic container chocked full of half-finished rolls and fruit and all kinds of tasty stuff.

"You're not supposed to be here," she said.

"Where am I supposed to be?"

"Nowhere—anywhere—but not *here*."

"You don't think I have money? I have money, but it's going for my tuition, and I'm just like you—trying to make through the u," I said, calling the university the 'u' like I heard other students say, just to show her I was up with her lingo.

"What about it?" I said.

"I'm not supposed to do what you're asking—"

"Yeah, sure, but it'd take me like two seconds." I looked up and down the skywalk. "Hey look, no one's here."

"Do you want me to call security?"

I get that question sometimes. That's when you want to move on.

"No," I said, then started to walk away. "I just want somebody to be human."

I only took a couple of steps and I heard her say, "Wait a minute," and she flipped a latch on her side of the counter which let the half-door swing open, and before you knew it, I was rummaging around down there, and found a couple of pieces of raisin muffin, a half a pear, and a cookie somebody nibbled on, then threw away. All the time, she had her back to me pretending I wasn't there. Then I heard a snap. College girl popped open a paper sandwich bag and held it out for me. I filled it up as much as I could.

I took it right out the door and down to the creek. I sat on a rock and listened to the water sounds. Some magpies came around for hand-outs. The college kids feed 'em, so they're not afraid of people. Magpies are sassy. They dive at you and if they have a chance, they'll take your lunch. At least they operate in daylight. Night brings the raccoons out. They'll eat anything. You have to be careful because if you get in their way, they'll attack. Newbies who sleep near dumpsters, find that out the hard way. I knew somebody once who was new to street ways and thought she'd get first grabs on throw-outs, but the raccoons got in the way and she got cut up pretty bad. Anyways, I figured I can always go back to the artsy café in the library and hit up that sappy college girl for grub when I need it.


SOMEONE WAS STANDING over me.

When I looked up, I had to squint because the sun was in back of her. She was one of those county cops. Her hair was done up in a bun in back with a stick through it, and her badge said "Officer Arlene Sparke." She squatted down to talk to me.

Here it comes, I thought. The 'what cha' doing with your life' talk. Like the big sister I didn't know I had. The one I didn't want. And I didn't need. Happens all the time. They see a kid like me and they figure they're going to help them. But then, I was wearing my new gloves and thought maybe she was going to write me up or something, and that Dancey probably turned me in, just like he said he'd do.

When she asked me what I was doing, I told her the Jesus story.

"Have you seen him yet?" she asked.

"No," I just got into town, and I was getting ready to go over to the correctional center to get the visitors' rules. I'm sure Jesus put me on his visitors' list.

"Want me to check for you? I can do that if you want."

"Nah. I'm ok."

"There's usually a waiting period, but maybe I could arrange something."

Whenever somebody like a cop wants to do you a favor, it's time to move on.

"It's not unusual for transferees to wait for 30 days or more before they're permitted to see visitors."

"Sure, if you can get me in early, that would be great."

She smiled. "I'll make a call, but I won't know until later today. Where can I find you?"

"Around. Yeah, I'll be around. I can call you if you give me your number."

"Do you have a 'cell?"

"No, but I can always get to a pay 'phone."

She wrote her 'cell number down on a piece of paper, then said, "By the way, my name is Billie." She wanted me to call her Billie even tho' it says Arlene on her name badge, but her fellow officers—mostly men—like to call her Billie. Then she smiled again.

One part of me said, "She just wants you to be ok, and she's a good cop." The other part of me said, "There'll be payback. Just wait."

Then she handed me five bucks and said, "Stay safe."

IT WAS MY DAY all right, my day for do-gooders. When I left the creek and walked around the side of the library, I saw an old lady in a wheelchair. She was trying to make it up the handicap ramp to the library. Her oxygen tube was dangling down and she was pawing at it but couldn't get to it. She looked all tired out. Then we made eye contact.

That was a mistake. Be aware of the things around you—I have to remind myself— glance around now and then, but walk fast, keep your eyes down. I should know better. Her face looked thick and solid white, like melted wax.

I helped her with her breathing tube, then she said, "My battery ran out," and gave me that helpless look again.

She promised me if I pushed her home—she lived down the block—I'd be an "angel." That's right, her angel.

I got her home all right. Turns out, she had worked as a nurse all her life, mostly for social services. Soon as she was ok, she started asking the questions. "Where are you from? What are you doing in town?" But I didn't tell her much. I said, "I'm visiting friends here, that's all."

Then she wanted to give me something.

"I don't need anything," I told her.

She insisted. "There," she pointed, "on the mantel there are some figurines. See them? You may take one. Choose any one you like."

"I have to be going, but thanks anyways."

She wanted to know when she was going to see me again. Probably never, I thought. That's all I need, to get wrapped up with some cripple.

Then I said, "Oh, I'm around. I'm sure we'll meet up somewheres," but I just wanted to get out of her house. It was creepy. The air was stale and all that old stuff, it was like a time trap. The furniture was worn and the lamp shades had fringe on them. Her name is June. I call her "Old Grinder," because that's what her teeth do after she talks. It's like she's adjusting them.

On my way out I asked, "You live here alone?"

She nodded yes.

I thought, how could she live alone like this, without anybody else around to help her? Yeah, and she was ahead of my thinking my thoughts. "I have meals-on-wheels," she said, "and a friend from the center who comes over most evenings for an hour or two."

Old Grinder was talking about a community center for seniors in town. They send old people out to help other old people. I think she needs more help than that, but it's what she wants, I guess. I just wanted out of there.

I headed across town to the Safeway parking lot where the second-hand bins are, and looked through some of the throw-aways. If you find something, you have to sign for it. There's some guy watching you. I found a scarf. It was a long one and it was purple. So I signed for it. I signed, "Old Grinder." It looks cool too. I flip it around like I seen college kids do.

When I came back, Boog was gone. I figured he was probably out digging around for stuff. I took out my note that I made in the library on the name of the place where Jesus was—Colechester State Correctional Institution—a medium security prison mostly, probably the best of all the places he'd stayed over the years, which reminded me I should be calling Officer Billie. I still had the five she gave me, all

I needed was some change to make that call, but when I was ready to leave, Boog showed up.

He wanted to know what I'd been up to.

"Nuthin' much," I said. "Just getting to know the town, is all."

"Yeah. Being an Airdale makes it tough, huh?" he said, meaning I was on my own. It's when you don't travel with other transies, or hang with them to learn about what's goin' on. I call people like me transies because I'm not a gutter punk or a panhandler, or a dog, or some kind of bum. I'm here, and then I'm there. Like that. And I don't like the word homeless either. I have a home in my heart. So my home's wherever I go. Jesus is in there too—in my home plan. We'll stay wherever we want when we get to Phoenix, but there's some great places along the shore of the Salt river with big dead trees to stop the wind and moss too for good bedding and just about everything you'd want, and it's just a couple of miles from the city.

"I do all right," I told Boog.

"I bet you do."

He looked around. "Hey, we should think about later." Then he pulled out a new bottle of vodka, and his eyebrows went up.

"Yeah, well I don't think I want to do that," I said. I knew what he meant.

"Look, kid, you can hang around, you know? Use the tarp. I'll even rustle up the eats, but we share, you know?"

I knew what he meant by sharing. "I don't feel right about that," I told him. "It's like I'm cheating on Jesus."

He put the bottle away. "Then maybe you should think about movin' on."

"Yeah. When I'm ready."

"Well, if you're not cooperating, you know, if we're not doing things together, then I don't see how you can stay on with me."

I figured I paid my way already with Boog.

"Like I said, 'when I'm ready.'"

He chuckled. "No, honey, that's not the way it is."

"Yeah it is. You know you're messin' with a minor, right?"

He was quiet then. He was quiet for a long time. I think he was thinking.

"You telling me you're not 18?"

"Do I look 18?"

That seemed to change things. I mean, he grumbled and said he had to go meet some friends, and if I wanted to stay for another night or two that'd be ok, and he'd stay on his side of the tarp, but he said, "Just fair to tell ya' kid, I never know when I'm movin' on. You might come back some night and find I pulled stakes."

"Fine with me."

"I didn't know it then, but I'd need Boog to help me spring Jesus early. Part of a plan cooked up by Officer Billie.

The next morning I got to the bookstore on the mall and they let me make my call. Billie had it all worked out. I could see Jesus in two—three days tops—but she wanted to go over some details with me. Said she could swing around by the mall for a chat.

I DIDN'T EVEN KNOW her. She showed up in jeans and a sweatshirt, and her hair wasn't in a bun either, held in with that stick. The natural look. Her hair was long and bouncy around her shoulders. She looked like a different person.

"Yeah, I was a runaway too," she began soon as we took one of those benches on the mall next to some shops. That's what they do when they want something: they tell you how much they're just like you.

"Yeah? Where?"

She said she ran away in St. Louis when she was a kid like me, but found the streets were harder than her home life, so she went back. "You could probably do the same thing," she told me.

What she doesn't know is, there's no back.

"You must have parents," she said.

This put me on the edge and she could see it too, and that's why she said we could get some lunch and I might feel better. We could talk things over. Another big sister come on.

We went to one of the mall restaurants, funky-country-hip, where the trust fund babies go. Officer Billie held the door, but I wanted to stay outside. We found a table on the patio and it was under one of those aluminum propane outdoor heaters. The soup of the day was "Veggie Lentil." Came with crusty bread too—for dipping.

It didn't take Billie long to come around to the subject again. She wanted to know about my parents.

I cut her off—"Look, are you getting me in to see Jesus, or what?"

"Sure I am. You know that."

"Sure," I said, like I didn't really take her word. "And what else? What else do you want?"

"I want to know about your family."

She was going to keep this up anyways no matter what, so I gave her something. I gave her the pool story.

Whenever I have to—and I don't like to do it either—but if I'm really pushed, I use this one: my dad is somewhere, but no one knows where. Even social services can't find him. He ran off when my mom went looney.

We lived in suburb of Phoenix. Lots of pools in Phoenix. It gets hot there and everybody wants to go for a cool dip. My mom took me and my sis' to a neighbor's house to play in their backyard pool. I was inside with some kids while mom was busy talking to one of the neighbor ladies—they were fixing lemonade or something—then people started shouting and running around. An older kid had my 'lil sis' out of the water, pumping her gut. She never came around.

My mom went to pieces, and never got it together after that. It went on for months. Dad couldn't take it anymore. I was sent to live with an aunt, but it didn't work out. She was mean and never wanted me in the first place. So I drifted around a lot, until I met Jesus. Since then, I've been following him around. We have an agreement when he gets out. We'll be together forever.

I waited for Billie's reaction, see if she took it. She just stared at me.


SHE'LL NEVER KNOW the real story. The real story is this: I was born behind a bunch of stores in a delivery area in an alley, then stashed in a dumpster. One of the stock workers came out to flatten some cardboard boxes so they'd fit in the dumpster, and he heard me crying.

My mother was found about a block from where I was born. Same alley. Anyways that's what a social worker told me when I was older, like 12. She said my mom died in childbirth. No one even claimed the body. I guess she couldn't go anywhere, a hospital or anything, mainly because she didn't want me anyhow. Who would throw their kid in a trash bin? Who'd do that?

The social worker—the one who told me the real story—said about two million kids are homeless. Most never leave the state where they were born. Some are like me, runaways. They've been abandoned, one way or another, and they usually die of exposure unless they're like the baby my friend left in a Taco Bell bathroom in Albuquerque. A little girl, I think.

Every year there are thousands of babies like that. I guess the social worker was trying to make me feel better. I was passed around from one place to another. It never worked out. Some of the families were ok, but there was always fighting, especially if they had kids already. Then the last home I was in, before I hit the streets for good, was run by a couple for government money. They had an online business on the side, selling car parts, garden equipment, whatever we could find or steal. They sent us kids out, kept us all in line, and nobody on the outside knew what was going on. They're still up to it as far as I know.

"How's the soup?" Officer Billie asked.

"Ok. But it could use some meat."

"It's probably better for you the way it is."

I could see she had other things on her mind, the way she dipped her spoon back and forth, like she was trying to line up what she was going to say.

"Look, I may have something you might be interested in. It could help you, and it could help the department," she said, meaning the other cops.

She paused, like she wanted me to know this was serious.

Ok, here it comes.  I just knew it.

"You see, there's a growing number of kids—" she stopped dipping her spoon and the handle clinked against the side of the bowl—"*kids* who are getting heroin.  We know some of the local pushers, but we need to find the source—the supplier, and where the supplier is getting the product."

This wasn't sounding good.  If I ever learned anything, it's stay away from drugs, and you never want to get in the way of pushers and addicts, and never ever get involved with dealers.

"You could help in a big way," she went on.  "We want you to consider—no one's rushing you, understand?  But just consider befriending someone who's been trading, maybe you can pose as an addict yourself, but get into the confidence of some of the pushers, maybe you could learn something that could help us apprehend whoever supplies the distributors.  Think you'd be interested?"

"Nope.  Not interested," I said, wiped my mouth, wadded up the napkin and threw it in the empty bowl.

"What if I told you that if we get information we can use, that takes us somewhere, it'd be possible to get an early release for Jesus."

I'd do anything for Jesus.  "How early?"

"Maybe as much as 60 days before his scheduled release date.  That would get you two together and you could get an early start to Phoenix and get set up for those nice winters they have down there."

She knew our plan, which was to go to Phoenix just as soon as he's sprung.  I thought maybe she'd been talking to Jesus.

"What do you want me to do?"


MY MEETING WITH JESUS came up before I knew it.

The guards even let us sit near each other in a common room with a table between us. He looked great—I mean his hair was all slicked back, and he was getting along with the other prisoners. No one hit him up to join a gang. He couldn't get over it; thought it was crazy, never heard of it before. There were gangstas around, sure, but he just had to stay away from them. He said they should have sent him here ten years ago. It would have been better for everybody. But things don't happen like that in the justice system. Can't expect them to make sense *and* be human.

Officer Billie told me not to tell anybody about our deal, about springing Jesus early, if I went along with her investigation, so I didn't say anything during our visit. Someday I will. When we're together. I'm the only one on his visitors' list, probably because what's left of his family can't get up here for one reason or another. Anyways, that's what he told me—that I was the only one. I didn't know it then, but I wasn't the only one. Jesus put somebody else on his visitors' list besides me.

Officer Billie was waiting for me when I came out. She was standing right there in the corridor. She wanted to know how it went—my meeting with Jesus.

"Fine," I said.

"That's good to hear. I'm glad you had a chance to visit. He seems like a nice young man, and I'm sure after this experience is behind him, he'll find his way, you know?"

"Sure," I said, but what she didn't know was that Jesus should never have been in prison in the first place, and it's not just the same old story every con cooks up, either. It's for real. If I did tell her the real story, she probably wouldn't believe me anyhow.

THAT AFTERNOON I WENT BACK to the surplus store, hoping to find Dancey. He wasn't there. I hung around for a while, went around the back, and I was about to leave when a car pulled up. Big black sedan with lots of shiny chrome. It was Dancey and another guy in the back seat. He got out, shook hands with the guy, and saw me standing there.

"What do you want?" he asked.

"I need money."

He laughed. "Yeah, ain't it the truth now."

"I'm serious. I'm not messing around. I'll pass for you."

"You will, huh? Tell you what, I'll give you the same deal I gave you before."

"Forget the part about turning me in. No one's going to care about the stuff I took," and I was thinking about Officer Billie and how she'd get me out of that one if I needed her to.

"Yeah, just do right by me and you'll be ok. We'll do a trial run. I'll put you onto a user, you deliver, bring back the cash, and you get paid."

"How much?"

"You get paid in trade, kid."

He meant product. "I don't do coke," I said.

"Coke?" he laughed. "It's not coke. It's heroin. Do heroin?"

I shook my head.

"Don't tell me you're clean?" he laughed. "Never took a hit? Not one?"

"I don't use the stuff."

"I don't believe you."

"So you don't believe me. So what? Try me out, see if I don't pass your stuff and come through for you. Give me 10 percent of what I bring back."

"Five. But don't ever go light on the cash, kid. You go light on me, and you won't be able to pass anything, ever again. Get it?"

"Yeah, I get it."

And that's how it started. Before I knew it I was delivering junk all over town: college dorms, private homes, and to "Buddy," some kid in his late 'teens maybe, who was selling to middle-school kids. That bothered me, but then I knew Officer Billie would nail him sooner or later, especially if I helped out. Plus, I was getting closer to Jesus all the time.

Every so often, I'd meet Billie in out-of-the-way places, like I'd bump into her on one of those trails around Chautauqua, or we'd meet at night near the cemetery. She thought it was important this way, face to face.

I told her about "Buddy" selling to school kids, and how she should arrest him. I gave her a description and where he hangs out— everything. She wrote it down in her cop notebook.

"We'll catch up with him, eventually," she said, "but we want to focus on the chain—like who's delivering to the guy you work for, and then get to the supplier."

"Yeah," I said, "I just know Dancey won't give me any info., and he's real intense about what I do. I can't get around him. If I did, and he found out, I don't know what would happen. Something bad."

"What if we supplied you with bait?"

"What kind of bait?"

"Cash bait. Let's say, you tell Dancey someone put you onto a buyer who wants a big purchase, but for that kind of money doesn't want to pay street, wants a discount. This buyer wants to deal with the supplier, the guy who has dealers like Dancey all over the southwest. That guy."

"Yeah, but there's probably another guy in back of him," I said.

"That could be, and we may never get to him. But maybe, if we can cut supply lines, disrupt the operation, we might be able to get some time to identify who's coordinating the shipments, actually running the organization. Either way it goes, we'll be taking drugs off the streets."

That's when she gave me the plan.

I was supposed to convince Dancey about this buyer, and the buyer would be a Fed, some undercover agent in DEA who really knows his stuff. I'd have some bait money, 10K, and I'd make sure Dancey understood the buyer wanted a 150K buy.

But first I'd have to convince Dancey the deal's for real. That meant working with the narc. Somebody to go with me, and if somethin' went wrong, cover me, and the cash. Billie set up a meeting.

The next day, she borrowed another cop's personal vehicle, and we drove outside of town. We drove for miles.

Officer Billie turned down a dirt road and we drove until we came to a grove, and hidden behind the trees was another car and a guy standing next to it.

"You need to get in sync, you two, so it's a flawless performance. Trust is everything."

The guy had the getup all right. So he didn't look like a narc, not at first, but you can always tell. There's always a give-away. I looked him over.

"No way," I said.

"What?" Officer Billie looked surprised. "I can give you every certainty that this officer has many successful drug busts, and is qualified beyond question—"

"Teeth," I said.

"Teeth?"

"Yeah, just look at 'em. They're perfect. He could be on a T.V. commercial. That's not all. Look at his face. It should have creases from too much sun and bad weather, knockin' around, you know? And his nails—not cracked or anything. He's supposed to be my backup man, right? I can't chance it. He'll mess it up. Dancey will spot him faster than I did. Less than a minute. I need somebody that looks like a transie, somebody that's real, not a half-stepper. I need Boog."

"Who?"

"A friend. You can trust him. He's big too, like a body guard. I'll be ok, and I'll get your money back too—all of it. All I need is a bottle of vodka—the good stuff."

"You're asking me to buy liquor?"

"It's for the sting," I said. I figured she'd like my cop lingo, and she'd want to get the hootch.

Officer Billie shook her head all the way back to her ride.

Soon as we got back to town, she pulled into a liquor store and bought the bottle. She reached in the back seat and gave me a back pack and told me to bring it with me the next time we'd meet.

IT DIDN'T TAKE LONG. The next day Officer Billie met me at the student union in the big square when the bell tower was chiming noon, and the place was crawling with students.

She brought another back pack, just like the one she gave me. We set them down on a bench, side by side, and made small talk for a while.

Then she said, "There's a dye packet in with the bills, so if the bait's tampered with, or gets mishandled, the bills can't be circulated. The money won't do anyone any good. Just show him the bills, but don't let him go through them."

We switched back packs, and soon as I showed up at the park, I told Boog, "We're going downtown. There's somebody I want you to meet," and gave him as much information as I could.

At first he wasn't too enthused about it, but I persuaded him. I told him about the junk the kids were using, and how helping Officer Billie would help me to spring Jesus early.

"I don't care about kid dopers, and I don't care about your deals, and I don't care about Jesus so you can forget it."

I showed him the bottle. That clinched it, even though I was ready to bring up other things, but I didn't have to; it looked like he knew he had to help me out on this one.

"You don't let anybody mess with this," I said, holding up the back pack. "And if there's trouble, I want you to protect the bait."

IT DIDN'T TAKE LONG to find Dancey. I explained the deal, and Boog was right behind me all the time I was talkin'.

Dancey wanted to see the cash—"earnest money"—he called it, so I zipped open the pack and he looked it over, pulled back the side just to see the stack of bills, then I closed it up.

"Look, kid, everything goes through me. You should know that. There's no meeting with my boss."

"What's goin' to happen when your boss finds out you passed up on 150K?"

"How's that gonna' happen?"

"It always happens. It's the grapevine. You can't keep any secrets from him, right?"

Dancey stroked his beard. He kept going over and over it like it would help him somehow. When he was done thinking it through, he said, "All right, I'll get the word to him. No promises. He might not go for it."

"When will you know?"

"Soon. Until then, I'll take that—" he said, reaching for the bag, "—for earnest money."

I jerked it back and handed it off to Boog. "No. That stays with me, for now," I said.

Boog and me, we started walking backwards, still facing Dancey, all the way until we got to the street.

I split with Boog when we hit the first intersection. Just down the block there was Officer Billie waiting outside a drugstore, just like we planned. She opened the back pack, checked the bills, then zipped it shut, slung it over her shoulder, and patted me on the head.

"Good job. Things should go smoothly from now until the bust. You can see Jesus again if you want, just let the administrative office know when you want to go over."

IT WAS A CLOUDY NIGHT, and not too cold if you kept moving. I didn't want to go back to the park right away, so I walked in the direction of where the college kids hang out—on 'the hill.' I was feeling pretty good; things were working out, and Officer Billie was confident about her big bust.

I spotted one of those cafés that had aluminum outdoor heaters, and pulled a chair up to one, and ordered a double hot chocolate. About the third sip in, I looked up and saw a black sedan pull up to the curb, stop for a moment, then pull out onto the street again. It was the same car that I saw Dancey get out of. I didn't know how to figure it. Maybe I was being tracked, and they—probably gangstas who worked with Dancey—wanted me to know they were keeping an eye on me. Maybe they thought they could follow me to the money, like I'd have it, but what did they know? All I could think of was this: if I got up and walked away, would they be waiting for me just down the street?

I stayed at my table for a long time. I guess I fell to sleep.

"MISS?"

I felt a nudge.

"Miss?"

It was the manager.

"We're closing now. I have to ask if you would visit us on another occasion."

It must have been midnight. The street was empty. I didn't want to go back to the park. It was just too risky.

So I cut through back alleys, crept in shadows alongside of homes, making sure nobody was following me, and before I knew it, I was on Old Grinder's street.

Her house had one light on. It must have been in the living room. I figured it was a night light, and she probably went to bed hours ago.

I snuck around back. Grinder has an old single-car garage that she keeps locked up, and I went around to a window on one side, took my jacket and wrapped it around my elbow, made a fist, then with my other hand, pushed against my fist until my elbow broke the glass and I heard a soft cracking sound, then I carefully took out each piece and set it on the ground not to make any noise, and crawled inside. There's lots of garden equipment in there, a push mower that's rusted and probably wasn't used for years, and shelves of old paint and tools and stuff. There's some clay pots on a bench, and they're covered with a sheet of plastic. I grabbed that, and curled up under the workbench. The place was warmer than I thought. Whoever was following me around would never find me here.

When I woke up the next morning, the first thing I wanted to do was to make it over to the book store and use their 'phone to call Officer Billie and let her know about why I ended up here, and not the park last night, but something came up.

I was easing myself back out of the garage window when I heard a voice: "I knew it. I knew somebody was in there."

Sure enough, it was Old Grinder. She was in her electric wheelchair and had a gun in her lap. She'd come down the ramp on her back porch. She must have glanced out her kitchen window when she was making breakfast and saw me trying to make it out of her garage.

"If you had knocked on the front door, like any self-respecting person might have done, why you could have stayed in my guest room," she said.

"It was very late, June," I said, trying to win her over. "And I didn't want to disturb you." Then I gave her my sheepish look.

"Well, as you can see, I'm prepared for intruders," she said picking up the pistol from her lap. "It's so old it probably won't fire anyhow," she chuckled, then slid it in a bag alongside of her wheelchair.

"C'mon now," she said, "you must be hungry. I have biscuits and eggs. How does that sound?"

"Yeah, ok," I said, "but I can't stay long. I have things to do in town."

When we were in the kitchen, she said, "It seems like you're going through a lot of trouble. And what might that be about, may I ask?"

I couldn't say anything.

"All right, then. Tell you what, as long as you're not a fugitive, or evading the law, you can stay here. I just want to make sure you're not up to no good."

That seemed like a fair trade: I tell her what she wants to know for a place and eats. "But I won't be here for long. You should know that up front, and I can help you a little, now and then, but I'm not taking care of you—"

"—Didn't ask you to—"

"Yeah. I know. And I don't want your guest room. I'll sleep in the garage. That's fine with me."

That's when I told her about Jesus, and why I followed him up here, and that we'll be together soon. "My friend—" I called Jesus my friend because I didn't want her to think I was hooked on him or anything because she might think there's somebody more important in my life than her.

"And just why is your friend serving time?" she asked.

"My friend's from a town outside of Phoenix, a place called Greenville Station. It's not much of a place, but it was his home. When he was a senior in high school, he'd go to desert parties. All the kids did. There's lots of dry washes out there where you can't see the partying going on. The kids kept switching the places around to confuse the cops. The cops love to bust 'em too. It's how they get their kicks.

There's some deep washes out there and they'd take one of the dirt roads, park off to the side and walk to where they couldn't be seen. Lots of alcohol and goofing around, but there's meth and ecstasy too, and any other drug that's available.

My friend had a few beers. All the kids did. But somebody brought tequila, blue agave, the good stuff. If he'd just stuck with the beer, he'd be ok, but he didn't. Then Carla showed up. They'd been dating so I guess she was kind of his girlfriend, but he was never serious about her. He told me. Carla was a senior too, and lived with her mom. Her dad was still in Mexico. She came out with some of her pom friends and stayed for a while, but soon as the party started to get rowdy, the girls she came with—the pom girls—wanted to get back, so she left with them. That was her mistake.

My friend's mistake was that he drove back later, by himself. But the rest of what happened is weird, and it shouldn't have happened at all.

He took the old dirt road back to town, but when he hit the fork, instead of veering off toward Greenville Station like he was supposed to, he drove up Route 89 towards Phoenix.

He must have been out of it. I mean, he ran a red light—that's what the police report said—and slammed into the side of another car that was making a turn. The impact was so bad, it rolled the other car three times.

The driver survived with minor injuries, but the passenger was in bad shape. She was in a coma when she was admitted to the hospital. If she died, the prosecuting attorney said it would be manslaughter. Here's the weird part: on her hospital report, her blood sample showed 11 times the amount of meth anybody could take and still be expected to survive. So she was a junkie anyways. On top of that, she was pregnant. Yeah, she was, like five months. Can you believe that? Her kid would have been an addict. Just like her, no good.

So I always thought she didn't think much about her own life, and going out like that wasn't such a bad thing. She would have ended up bad any way you want to look at it. Her kid, too. I just know. Her, and her kid, they were wasted from the start.

Nobody understands how my friend came out of it. His car was totaled. It's funny, because he remembers the party, what he drank, and being with Carla and her friends, but the rest is a blur. He doesn't remember taking the wrong fork, or running the red light, or what happened afterwards.

He was in the hospital for a couple of weeks. His brain swelled up from the concussion, and they thought he might not come out of it. Eventually, the swelling went away, and when he came around, he was interviewed by the cops. Soon as he was able to stand, they took him to a holding facility. The next day he had his hearing. That's when he learned about all the charges against him.

His family couldn't afford an attorney, so the one appointed by the state was a half-step. He wasn't even around when my friend was given his interview for the sentence that's recommended to the court. He should've been there to persuade the people who did the evaluation to reduce the sentence they'd give the court. But he didn't. He was off somewheres else.

I mean that girl that died, she wasn't any good. She would have killed herself anyways. But that's not what the court said—the judge is the court—and my friend was sentenced to more time than he deserved. He took a big hit. That's the way I see it."

Old Grinder listened to every word. "You must be a loyal friend," she said. "It's good when you care about others."

"Look, I have to go do that business in town," I told her. I really wanted to check in with Officer Billie, and to see if Boog was at the park, too. About now, I figured he was wondering what I was up to, not that he was missin' me, but maybe, maybe he was wondering what happened after we split up at that intersection last night.

When I got to the park, Boog wasn't there. His tarp, bed roll, everything, gone, just like he'd never been there in the first place.

At the time, I couldn't understand why he upped and flew out of there. Maybe it was like he said; that someday he'd pull up stakes and I wouldn't find him anymore.


THEY KEPT ME WAITING for the longest time.

After I'd signed in, they let me sit for more than an hour. Finally, a guard came out from the counter with the window with crisscrossed wires in it, and he had a clip board with him.

"You here to see . . . mmm . . . inmate Jesus . . . Jesus Amparo . . . del Rio?"

I said, "Yes," but I was worried, and I didn't know why. I just knew something was up.

It took another 10 minutes before they helped Jesus into the common room. He was busted up. It was hard for him to talk. He'd been in the infirmary overnight and he had a plastic cup with a cover and a straw that he sipped through to get his water in him. His ribs were bruised, and he was bandaged up, and his throat was dry from medication. He could barely whisper.

Nobody knew why he was jumped. He just was. That wasn't good enough for me. When you get hit in prison, there's always a reason.

It had to been a set up. The only thing I could come up with was that Dancey's drug pins learned about Officer Billie and me and the bust. But where would they get that kind of info? It took me a while to figure, then it came to me: it was Boog. I didn't tell Boog everything, but enough to get him to go with me to Dancey's and protect me and the money, instead of a narc who would have messed up. Yeah, and I told him that I was waiting for Jesus to get out.

The guys in that black sedan that spotted me the other night must have beat it out of him. They wanted me first, I guess, because I had the bag of dough; probably followed us until we split up, then when they saw I was going to stay at the restaurant, they went after Boog. Once they knew I was in on it, they got their thugs to work on Jesus from the inside.

Jesus got beat up because of me.

I called Officer Billie and left a voice message: "I'm not in with you anymore. Not now. They got Jesus—bad. And it's all because of you, you thinking we could outsmart dealers. No way. I guess that never happens, and I shouldn't have thought it would. But I'm out, I mean, what good is Jesus if he's dead?" Then I screamed some shit at her.

The rest of the day I spent back at Old Grinder's garage, thinking.

Just before night came around, I made a quick trip to the mall and made another call to Officer Billie. This time she answered. She wanted to see me, right away.

We met outside the Chautauqua dining hall near the foothills. Billie brought a blanket, and spread it out on the ground.

We sat there and just talked for a long time. They never got to the dealer in Denver like they wanted. The whole bust was called off as soon as they knew the big dealer's guys got the info out of Boog.

"You tried," she said, "we all did. It happens that way sometimes. Things just don't go the way they're supposed to." She put her hand out like she was going to brush back my hair or something. I pulled back.

"I'm sorry," she said.

Then she told me Boog was in county general—she meant the hospital—and he had gone back to the park after our bait meet with Dancey, packed up and was heading out of town when the supplier's guys caught up with him. I guess they gave up on waiting for me outside of the restaurant, and spun around to find Boog.

"You can see him, if you want. I can arrange that."

"You arranged enough. I don't want to see Boog. I want to see Jesus."

"I'm afraid that's no longer possible."

"What do you mean?"

"I mean, you've been taken off his vistors' list."

"Why?"

"I'm not sure," she said and tried to smile, but it was a sad smile. He's been having visits from another person. Did you know that?"

"No."

"Do you want to know?"

"Tell me."

"Someone by the name of Carla Montoya. Do you know Carla?"

"No."

"I'm sorry, but when an inmate removes a visitor from his list, there's really nothing we can do."

I didn't blame him. He knows I messed up, and if I could trade places with him, I wouldn't want to see me, either. He keeps up with me, and he might get hit again. That could happen too.

If Jesus didn't want me anymore, then I wanted to hear it from him. The only way to do that was to hang around until his release. So I decided to do that. I had options too—I could go back and shine with Annie, or I could put up at Old Grinder's place. She offered me a deal: I could stay with her and finish a GED, then go to community college and "make something" of myself. She doesn't understand anything, sometimes.

IT WAS A LONG, SLOW summer. I spent a lot of time at the university; I'd sit on the quad for hours just watching the students. And I didn't spend every night at Old Grinder's either. Sometimes I'd sneak off and sleep in the stairwell by the old church, or in a space I found behind a brick pile in the back of an abandoned house, and once, I slept on a roof of an empty building where nobody'd bother me. That way I wasn't around her all the time, and I could do different stuff and hang out where I wanted.

The last thing I asked Officer Billie for, was Jesus' release date. They gave him another two months for being in a fight, even though it wasn't his fault, and he was the one that got broke up. They don't care. He wouldn't be out until November. Once Billie got me the date, I figured I'd show up and talk to him personally. Maybe we could work things out.

THE BIG DAY ARRIVED. I came extra early and stayed around the fence by the release gate. I knew Jesus would be coming through it soon enough, and we'd finally have our chance to be together.

It was cold, and I wore my mom's sweater and my purple scarf I got from charity, and I could see my breath. I wore my gloves, and I walked up and down the fence line with my arms folded, trying to get warmer.

About noon, a car drove up. It looked like a sports car—flashy— and the only person in it was the driver. Then I had a chilly feeling that made me do a dry choke.

She looked about the right age, and she was all fixed up too, make-up and everything. It must be her, I thought, it must be that Carla person.

She just left the motor running and stayed inside, staring out her window at the gate.

Finally, it happened. The officer escorted Jesus from the building door to the fence, said something to him, shook his hand, and unlocked the gate.

He didn't take two steps before she was on him. I mean, soon as she spotted him, she jumped out of her car and ran up to him and hugged him and wouldn't stop. I couldn't get near them. She beat me out.

Then he kissed her. After he did, he looked down the fence, as if he was looking at me. That was all. They both walked fast to the car laughing and talking. I guess they seemed like they were glad to see each other.

Even after they left, I could smell her perfume in the air. It wouldn't go away.

Like I said, I have options. But I'm not going to school like Grinder wants, or go back to shining with Annie. I just don't want to, that's all.

When I got back to the garage, I thought for a long time. I thought how warm it must be out on the bottoms, that Salt River bank outside Phoenix where there's lots of moss to keep warm in. Who knows? Maybe Jesus will get tired of Carla. She looks like a lot of work anyways. And maybe someday I'll find him on the river, where we belong. In the meantime, there might be some other kids like me out there living on the banks.

# RED-EYED PIGEONS

HE WAS WAITING in the Marais district, in Place des Vosges, the oldest square in Paris, for one of the public homes to open so he could finally meet another giant like himself.

Clio, his new-found traveling companion, was off window shopping. They had left the hotel early, finding it impossible to sleep simply because they were both too excited, and when they arrived, most of the stores were still closed.

Clio would return in a few minutes and they would make the visit together. The walk from the hotel, even though it was only a few blocks, was not easy for him, so he rested on a green bench by a fountain, and stared at the pigeons that pecked at the crumbs tossed to them by children and their *au pairs*.

Paris was unreal; a place he would have never visited himself, never in his lifetime, or did he have any desire, that is, until recently. His new condition made it all possible, still, it was a long way from home, where only a few months before, he was living out a modest retirement from his work as an assistant manager of a bottling plant in suburban Philadelphia, with his wife, Marguerite. Everything considered, he was satisfied, more or less, that is, until his body began to change.

It was during an otherwise routine act, when Walls first noticed his phenomenon, the one that would create for him a new future. He was cutting his toe nails and realized he had done the same thing only days before. And it wasn't just his nails, but his hair.

Marguerite brought up the subject.

"Are you using something?" she asked at breakfast one morning.

Her husband was buttering his toast, and looked up, "Using?" he repeated.

"Yes, something on your hair. That little bald patch on the back seems to have filled in."

"No. I've done nothing unusual," he replied.

Walls—everyone called him that—was his last name and no one seemed to use his first name which was Anthony, only his wife, and then it was on rare occasions, and she would say, Antonio, whenever she wanted his attention. She would say it softly, with affection.

After she mentioned his hair at breakfast, Walls became increasingly aware of his body. He began to examine it daily, noticing the texture of his skin, the size of his pores, the thickness of his eyebrows, and it wasn't long before something truly significant happened.

Every morning, before getting out of bed, Marguerite hugged him. It was routine. She would put her arms around him and press the side of her face into the hollow of his chest. The morning following the breakfast talk, she did the same thing she had done for years, then watched him as he stood, walked over to get his robe, and noticed his pajamas. The bottoms were raised above his ankles, so much so that it caught her attention.

Marguerite threw back her covers and went straight to her sewing area which occupied a corner of the second bedroom of their apartment, and rummaged around until she came up with a cloth measuring tape. She took this to their bedroom and asked her husband to stand up straight with his back against the wall. She ran the tape from his head to his heel, made a note that she would use as a reference, and a few days later, took another measurement. No change.

After a week had gone by, Marguerite took another, and found he had gained nearly an inch in height. By the second week, he had grown an additional inch and quarter, and at that point, she insisted he see their physician.

Walls didn't go. Instead, he called his friend Auggie, a former co-worker from the bottling plant. They met every week—usually Wednesdays, when there wasn't a crowd—at a sports bar in a local mall that featured an electric arcade. There they played the games, accumulated prize coupons and redeemed them for novelty items: plastic watches, stuffed animals, puzzles, tin flutes, and cheaply-made miniature compasses. Walls turned his share over to Auggie since he had no grandchildren himself, and they might have a beer, sometimes a sandwich in the sports bar. They would watch golf or football on television, talk off and on, and before long they passed away most of the afternoon.

Before leaving, they asked for any scraps from the kitchen, and later, on their way home, they would feed the pigeons in the park. The birds pecked at anything held out to them, and once, Walls noted their coloring—the iridescent feathers around their necks—that shown in the sun.

"They're fat," Auggie said. "They eat too much and they look like they've been up all night." It was then, at that moment, that Walls explained his medical condition to Auggie.

"We get a little older," he shrugged, "and we get out of shape. Things change," Auggie laughed.

They looked at each other.

"You buyin' it?"

"Buying?" Walls asked.

"What I just said."

"Not really."

Auggie laughed again. "To be honest, you didn't have to tell me. I mean, it's obvious as hell, you know?"


WHEN WALLS RETURNED home, his wife asked him about his visit to their physician.

"He didn't say much. Wants to see me next week," then he went to his room, removed his shoes, and looked at his swollen feet. He had been wearing a pair of rubber athletic shoes with most of the front cut away to accommodate his toes, and there were blisters along the sides of his feet.

Eventually, he brought himself around to seeing the family doctor who suggested a specialist in growth disorders.

"A pituitary malfunction is my best guess. But yours is a case of delayed onset, which is anomalous. That is, I've never seen a man your age experience something like this," and sent him to see a neuroendocrinologist, Dr. Pierpont.

He couldn't get in right away; Pierpont's referrals were being held up for some reason, and by the time he came in for his appointment, another two weeks had passed. None of his clothes fit. His wife bought him size 15 EE oxfords at the second-hand Big and Tall shop, and he could barely fit into them. When he did meet with the specialist, he was examined, and Pierpont made notes as he went along.

"I want you to take a few tests over at the university medical center. I'll schedule them, and soon as the results are in, we'll meet and discuss your best options. How's that sound?"

Anthony Walls left Dr. Pierpont's office with a list of tests and dates. Marguerite drove him to the medical center three days that week, where they spent several hours at a stretch, and at the end of the testing, he was exhausted, and complained his legs ached. She called Pierpont who explained that her husband's condition creates rapid and abnormal bone growth, and as a result, "an attendant disposition to pain."

He prescribed some anti-inflammatory medication, and told her she could bring her husband in the next day because the test results were in, and he wanted to speak with him personally—a consultation.

"I've always found that in a situation as unique as yours," he began, "the best approach is to speak directly about the facts. In cases like yours, Mr. Walls, the news is rarely promising. If you were younger, say in your 'teens, and the growth rate was less, we might attempt surgery. But as you know, we are well past the age of such an opportunity, and this restricts our efforts considerably, I'm afraid. With medication and radiation therapy we hope to reduce the production of growth hormone and we may see a cessation for short periods, but overall the condition will continue to deteriorate."

"Deteriorate?" Marguerite asked. "Do you mean it will get worse? That he will keep on growing?"

"Exactly," Dr. Pierpont said.

"Then what?" she asked.

"Well, whenever we come to a critical juncture, we can discuss options at that time."

Walls seemed to be hearing little of the conversation. His mind had gone elsewhere.

"We have to know what to expect, Doctor," Marguerite pleaded.

Pierpont sighed. "I wouldn't look at this all at once. Take it in small doses."

"We have to prepare ourselves," Marguerite insisted.

Pierpont, seeing she was determined, gave in, but it was with reluctance.

"Very well, then. The joint pain will extend to the bones of the legs and arms. Mr. Walls might experience a tingling sensation in his extremities, even loss of sensation, due to the inability of the heart to provide sufficient blood and oxygen. Eventually, the heart will become overworked. There could be some light headedness, congestion, shortness of breath, difficulty with mobility. But as we move along, we can address those complications with various medications, prosthetic devices and the like. That much is certain."

He smiled like someone trying to be confident. This was not shared by his patient, or by Marguerite.

"I must tell you," he said, looking over the steel frame of his glasses, "your rate of growth is uncommon even among the most severe hypotropic populations." Here, he tapped out a few key strokes on his computer and brought up charts of comparative patient data he'd been reviewing.

"In fact, in a matter of as little as two or three months, barring the unexpected, you may very well become the world's tallest human being."

Dr. Pierpont waited for a reaction. "How do you feel about that?"

Walls didn't know what to feel. Taken back by the doctor's information, his head was crowded with thoughts. Then he asked a strange question, which, over time, would become his main pursuit.

"Are there others . . . like me?"

"If you are asking if there are other patients afflicted with gigantism, why yes, although it's a rare pathology. Cases do come up, and they are scattered all over the world, and while there's some similarity in treatment, we find their therapies are unique to the individual, often supplemented with various treatments, and the use of online support groups. We can recommend a list, if you like. Now, if you are asking about those who might experience your illness at your age, with your symptoms and growth rate, we must make special research efforts in that direction."

Sensing Wall's interest, Pierpont instantly decided to use it to help advance an idea he brought with him to the consultation and hadn't yet revealed. "I've been speaking with some of my colleagues at Mayo. They want to meet you. In fact, their research data banks are the best in the world and they can tell you if there are other cases like your own. Not only that, but where those patients are located, if it's possible to communicate with them directly, and so on. We will provide for your expenses during the observation period."

The mere suggestion of the possibility of finding others that shared his condition seemed to animate Walls. For the first time since the beginning of the consultation, he seemed genuinely intrigued.

At this point it was Pierpont's aim to further stimulate the enthusiasm shown by his patient. "We could place your inquiry into the study itself, make it a research priority. They only want to observe you, run a few tests. You will find the staff appreciative, and they will treat you with every dignity. Also," he added, with raised eyebrows, "if you accept, there will be a stipend. It's offered as an incentive."

"You mean," Marguerite said, "you want to pay my Antonio because he is a curiosity."

"Only in a medical sense, and to benefit your husband, and others who may suffer from a similar malady, of course. This is a positive prospect, Mrs. Walls, and I hope you regard it as such."

They left Pierpont's office bewildered by all the information. Over the next few days, Walls was booked into one of the better hotels near the Mayo Clinic. He had signed numerous medical papers, giving his permission for procedures, consultations, and other commitments not completely clear to him; follow-up testing, a schedule of visits with various specialists, and an agreement to submit to other procedures that may be necessary in the course of the disease.

By the time they returned home, Marguerite was already receiving invoices from Walls' first round of lab work. Their health insurer did not offer coverage. As the agent explained, "The tests are very rare, as is your husband's medication. Costs become greater, you see? Your husband's condition—and its treatment—are known in the health care industry as 'exotic.' I'm sorry."

Walls took to sleeping on squares of air foam Marguerite bought at a local camping outfitter, and attached the pieces together with fiber tape.

He had to duck now when entering doorways. His voice deepened, and when he spoke, it sounded as if his words were coming out of a dark cave. He experienced frequent headaches. At first, with all the testing, he had lost his appetite, but within a few days, it turned ravenous. Walls consumed everything in the refrigerator, and when Marguerite restocked it, the food only lasted a short time. Items she had put away for special occasions in the cupboards vanished. Marguerite turned to a food warehouse in town where she could buy in bulk.

The stipend promised by Dr. Pierpont never arrived. Marguerite made several inquiries. For some reason, the request for Walls' payment for participating as a medical subject didn't survive the business office used by the hospital for its financial operations. The business office labeled the request as "an inappropriate use of budgeted funds."

The bills were mounting, and Marguerite returned to her old job working at a local dry cleaners.

They didn't know how long they could remain in their apartment. It had become much too small, with a hundred inconveniences that made Walls' new life difficult, and at times, aggravating. It was impossible for him to fit in the shower. And since Marguerite was away most of the day working, she asked for a nurse assistant, but health care refused her request.

All this was about to change with Auggie's idea. During the course of a telephone call, and prompted by his wish to know more about his friend's health, he asked, "Why don't you do something with yourself?"

Walls was uncertain about what he meant, so he said, "I'm listening."

"There's a lot of people out there who are interested in people like you. They want to know about your disease, how you live, your plans, what will happen to you."

Auggie went on with his idea; he'd come over with his new camera and film Walls in his home, ask him questions, conduct a series of short interviews, "to keep them coming back for more," as he put it. "This could be big."

"Then what?" Walls asked.

"Then we'll put it on YouTube. You'll be a sensation," Auggie was quick to reassure him. "You have debts, right? And your debts are getting worse, aren't they? Is that fair to Marguerite? You need a new apartment, new medical equipment, and so many other things now. Marguerite can't keep up, you know."

Auggie was convinced the video would attract hundreds of thousands, maybe millions of viewers. Something good would come of it. He was certain.

Walls considered the offer, and having no other prospects, or income to pay for his escalating expenses, agreed. His agreement came with a condition: "Marguerite can't know about this."

Such was the pact made among the retired bottlers.

Walls ended the 'phone conversation by saying, "Who knows, maybe this will help me find other people like me."

Auggie came over and filmed his friend when Marguerite was at work, posted it, and within a week there were thousands of hits. Some viewers searched out Walls' 'phone number and called his home. He quickly had the number changed, but not before answering two of the most important calls of his life.

One was from a publicist, and another from an agent who had already made inquiries on Walls' behalf, and all Walls had to do, the agent said, was to give the word and he would pay for his trip to New York for an appearance on one of the late night TV talk shows.

There were other commercial possibilities, one in particular, involved a fertilizer manufacturer in France that wanted Walls to represent the growth potential of their product—an amusing approach judging from the company's proposal—and he would be well compensated for his trouble.

When Walls hesitated, his publicist called personally to convince him to take the contract, and as an inducement, he added, "Maybe you didn't know this, but there are many giants in France."

With each day, more offers came in. Meanwhile, he was becoming a YouTube sensation.

"Our viewers want updates," Auggie told him. "They need to follow your progress," and he proposed weekly segments. "Listen to just how great this is becoming: there's a blog where viewers post their thoughts about you, and another site has a link to a gambling pool. They're betting on how tall you'll become. There must be offline betting as well. I'll have to look into that," Auggie mused.

"Is there anyone else like me?"

"Not *exactly* like you, but you never know. We have to keep going with this thing. Maybe will find others like you out there— somewhere."

"Will there be enough so Marguerite won't have to keep working?"

"Absolutely," Auggie confirmed, realizing as he said this, he had become his friend's business manager in every practical sense. He was already talking to the publicist and the agent about Walls' schedule.

All this was fine with Anthony Walls. With the money coming in, he could afford to move out of his apartment, and maybe even buy a house. The medical bills would be paid. Marguerite could quit her job. She would not come home smelling of dangerous dry cleaning chemicals. It was all looking up.


AUGGIE ARRANGED to travel into the city for his appearance on the late night show. They had managed to keep the information from Marguerite right up until the day before they were ready to leave.

It was during the evening, when Auggie—as the retirees agreed beforehand—would come over to explain the plan to Marguerite. After all, it would be for her welfare, as well. The television taping would be followed immediately with a transatlantic flight to France to film the fertilizer commercial.

Auggie spoke directly to Marguerite. "We have to take these opportunities as they come. If we hesitate, we could lose out." He then produced a file for appearances, endorsements and interviews, hoping she would be pleased.

"Why didn't I know about these . . . these *deals*?" she said.

"We wanted to make sure they were legitimate offers," Auggie said. "Besides, the New York appearance will be quick and easy, nothing to be concerned about. As for the commercial, that's a transoceanic flight, and we know how you feel about flying."

It was true. Marguerite abhorred flying, even for something as important as this.

"I don't agree," she said.

"What don't you agree with?" Auggie asked.

"All of it. My husband has to be a freak attraction so we can get out of debt. That's it, isn't it? Do you think he's ready to travel half-way around the world? Just look at him."

"I can do it," Walls said.

Marguerite went to her sewing room, took out a suitcase from the closet and began filling it with her clothes and personal items.

"Where are you going?" Walls asked.

"To my sister's place. Maybe it will give us time to think about what's really going on here. All of a sudden, Antonio, everyone wants to put you on exhibit, and I don't think we're ready for that, do you?"

When Marguerite was determined, as she was at this moment, there was little chance of changing her mind, Walls knew. After all, hadn't she been betrayed? No one had included her in planning the events that would affect her, and possibly alter her life.

When Marguerite announced she was leaving, Auggie became uncomfortable in the apartment, as if he had intruded in their affairs, and was now an unwanted guest. He took his file, shook Walls' hand, and left. Soon after, Marguerite followed, driving to her sister's home upstate.

Although Walls tried many times that night to call his wife, she had turned off her 'cell 'phone and he couldn't get through. Walls was sitting in the middle of the living room, dozing on and off, when a call came in. He thought it was Marguerite, but his anticipation shifted quickly when he learned it was Auggie.

"I've got it again," he said weakly. "Of all the times for this to happen, now's not it," and fumbled through an apology. It was a recurrent problem that came and went from time to time; an untreated pancreas prone to inflammation. It would have him doubled over for days.

Auggie managed to give Walls the travel information before he begged off, saying how sorry he was he couldn't accompany his friend as planned. "You have to go ahead. Do this for Marguerite," he said, and gave his last good-bye.


WALLS BOARDED THE ACELA at the 30th Street Station, taking the compartment Auggie reserved for him. He arrived in New York City in record time, with a chauffeur waiting to whisk him away for the talk show.

He was shown to the green room where the other celebrities waited until called to go on. There was the recent winner of a reality show who lost half her body weight, a mime who performed magic feats, a midget comic, and a model, who was, at the moment, staring at Walls.

"You're big," she said, and looked at him coyly.

Walls stared off across the room.

She came over and sat next to him. "Are you being interviewed tonight?"

"That's what I understand, yes."

"So you're just going to tell America about yourself?"

"Yes. But I want to ask if there's anybody else out there like me. Maybe someone will be watching."

"Why do you . . . want another . . . you?"

"I need to know. It would be better if I knew there was someone else like me."

"I see," she said, and held out her hand. "My name's Clio. I have an interview too. They want to ask me about how I lost my job. No one will hire me now, not since I had that affair with

_____," and here she named a well-known politician, a darling of his party, a senator. "They say I broke up his family and destroyed his career."

"I'm sorry for you then," Walls said.

"Look, why don't we meet after the show? I think we can do something that will be good for the both of us."

WALLS HAD NO INTENTION of accepting the invitation. Instead, after his segment, he left the studio to go directly to his hotel, but once out on the street, Clio seemed to appear out of nowhere, tugging on his sleeve.

"Hey, you," she said quietly, "I thought we had a date."

Walls noticed there were two other girls with her.

"We're going to a new club," she said, slipping her arm in his, "and we thought you might want to join us. It'll be fun. I want to introduce you to my friends," and the others laughed and seemed to be having such a good time, and asked him questions about his life—what it was like—and seemed to value him in some way he did not quite understand, and before long he found himself walking along with them, with more energy than he had in months, enjoying their company, their attention, and did not think once of returning to his hotel as he had promised himself.

Later, after they entered Pandora Club, ordered drinks, and Clio had shown him off to her friends, after they danced, that is, when Walls stood moving his hips and shuffling his feet slightly, Clio said,

"We both need the same thing. We need publicity. We'd be good for each other. A team, you know? What's your next gig?"

He mentioned the commercial contract for the French fertilizer company.

"Where in France?" she wanted to know.

"Paris."

"Paris? Do you know Paris? I do. I've been there many times. I could go with you, show you around."

And that was how Clio would revive her career and give Walls a new twist to help his image: being seen in the company of a young, and up to this point, successful model with her own public story. People couldn't help but wonder about such an unusual couple. They would be a sensation. Of course, it was all for show. Let people imagine what they want. That was the point, wasn't it? Popularity ratings would soar, and job opportunities were certain to follow.

On the flight from New York to Paris, Walls was escorted to the Premium Voyager cabin where Auggie had reserved a seat for himself, now occupied by Clio with some last minute reservation changes, and two for Walls. During most of the flight, he rested across the seats and listened to his favorite tunes that Marguerite loaded on his media player she had given him last year for Christmas.

Within a couple of hours, Clio roamed through the various sections of the plane, ordered drinks twice, flipped through several magazines, and finally, bored, turned to Walls, pulled out one of his ear buds, and held it so she could hear his music, mostly show tunes of the 50s and 60s.

"God, how can you listen to that creepy stuff?"

Within minutes, she flipped open her laptop, went online to a popular music site, downloaded hours of trendy hits—her music. "Here," she said, "now you have something worth listening to," and handed the device back to him.

Soon after checking into the fashionable five-star hotel in the fourth arrondissement which had "nearly everything," as Clio promised, they left by chauffeured van to take in some of the sights. They were free, on their own, until the following afternoon when he had to meet with the producers of the commercial.

The driver took them around the *Arc de Triomphe*, through the old quarter, then stopped so they could visit one of the shops located under the courtyard of the Louvre, where Clio hinted to Walls that she would like a scarf—she loved scarves and adored people who wore them. She selected a silk one with swirls of crimson, and was so delighted with it, she had to have another.

On one of the grand boulevards, about to enter an exclusive boutique, she was approached by a photojournalist and an assistant from French National Television. They had recognized Clio immediately. What was she doing in Paris? Had she seen the senator before they split? Had he contacted her? And who was her new companion?

Clio had them wait, returned to the van for a few words with Walls, then waved them over for a brief street-chat that would be shown on the weekly installment of "Who's Visiting Paris?" video magazine.

By the time they returned to their hotel, they were exhausted. Before retiring to their room, an ambassadorial suite no less, Walls visited the concierge's desk.

Walls remembered what his agent told him, and repeated it to the concierge: "There are giants in France. Where may I find these giants?"

The concierge, dressed in a dark suit with a subtle pinstripe, plaid shirt without a tie, an ensemble that Clio explained, "doesn't have to be stylish; its style is how it's worn, at least in Paris," seemed confused by Walls' question, but only for a moment, then he smiled, as if he had made a secret discovery.

"Monsieur, France is a land of giants. There are giants everywhere. I suggest you begin at Place des Vosges," and unfolded a map, and drew the route.

"Here," he explained, "simply go to the end of the vaulted corridor, and in this corner," he placed an X on the map, "you will find a giant, and you will learn of other giants as well."


AND THIS IS HOW the unlikely couple arrived at the oldest square in Paris early the next morning. Walls set himself down on a park bench, observed the children feeding the pigeons, noting how similar they were to the red-eyed pigeons he and Auggie fed in Franklin Square in Philadelphia on Wednesdays when they were together, when Clio returned from the shops just beginning to open, excited about a designer purse with matching shoes she had seen in a window, and had to have, just soon as they made their visit to the home of the giant.

They walked arm and arm through the vaulted arcade until they came to a marble plaque with gold lettering on the front of the building near the doorway that read:

# VILLE DE PARIS
## MAISON
## DE
## VICTOR HUGO

Immediately, Clio knew what this meant, and she wanted to spare her companion any disappointment.

"Tony," she said, "this may not be what you think."

By the time the words were out of her mouth, he had already entered, and was at the reception desk receiving a visitor's guide and a set of earphones.

They climbed the stairs together, an ungainly pair, she trying to steady him as he took each step, leaning against the thick, carved railing for support. When they arrived at the second floor, they found a spacious apartment with servants' quarters, a reception room with elegant furnishings and mid-nineteenth century décor. The rooms were rich with artifacts, paintings, and with the combination of heavy draperies, ornate wall paper and lighting, they gave off a dark warm, roseate glow.

Walls spotted a rosewood settee, and was about to seat himself, to wait for the giant, when one of the curators came over and said, "No, Monsieur, you must not," and waved him away.

"But where is the giant?" Walls asked. The man gestured toward a daguerreotype with some slight coloration added later, a bit of rouge to the cheeks, and eyes that appeared bloodshot. "He is one of France's great heroes," he said, "adored by the people."

"Are there other giants?" Walls asked.

"Certainly. Have you been to the Panthéon? Curie, Dumas, Zola, they are all there," and led Walls by his arm, to another room.

"Even the man who died in this bed," he used his open palm again, "Hugo himself."

When the guide saw his visitor was still in a state of disbelief, he added, "Is this not enough, Monsieur?" He tapped on the floor with his foot, determined to impress his guest, "These woods—how you say—planks? On these stood Liszt, Daudet, Gautier, Voltaire, and many others. Is this not enough?"


WALLS STOOD AT THE TOP of the wide staircase, leaning against the balustrade, not wanting to descend. Clio, in an attempt to renew the enthusiasm lost by her companion ran down a few steps.

"C'mon, Tony," she encouraged him, "there's lots to do."

He tried to follow, and when he saw her at the bottom of the stairs, he became short of breath, and could no longer trust his legs as they had gone numb, and he could not concentrate on anything, and would never hear Clio's request: "I want to go to Pére Lachaise. Its' not very far. We could walk." She wanted to see the niche of Isadora Duncan, one of her idols, she explained, "in the columbarium," but of course, Walls was by then, beyond her.

# FAN CLUB

LEAVE THE DOOR OPEN? Sure, I can do that. I know there are other students who will be here soon to see you, but I wanted to come extra early. This is a great way to take a final. Oh, before I forget, here's my paper. I think you'll like it. The idea of a student conference on the last night of class is—

What's that? Yes, I know it's supposed to be about the course— nothing personal—I get it, but it's hard to separate them in my case. You'll understand once I explain.

Usually this time of year I'm in Florida with my mom's family, but no change of fall colors like here. She calls them family even though she's not related because they've been so good to her over the years. Mom's been working for them since she was 19. They go down for the winter months, and come back to Brockport for the spring and summer. She does everything for them; the cooking, cleaning, and scheduling. They gave her enough money so she could get her own place here in town. They paid for my piano lessons, and that's why I could go to private school, and when things didn't work out, I got in at The Elysium Academy of Human Growth and Development.

I'm pretty much on my own now, but I can stay at my mom's place here in town whenever she's in Florida. She lets me do that because she feels guilty. So rather than hang around the house, I decided to take a couple of classes here at the college.

When mom started dating her new boyfriend—my dad split when I was just a little tot—she didn't want me around. Cramped her style, maybe. I'm not sure.

I was enrolled in Kingsley High my freshman year, in Honors no less, a really good private school, as you may have heard, and she didn't like that, so she had to invent reasons to get me out. She said I hit animals, beat them so bad they were nearly dead. Even had some neighbors lie for her. Said I went into rages, stole things from her. She really made me look bad.

My dad lives upstate—about as far north as you can go. He's Native American and French and he and my mom got married when they discovered I'd be coming into the world to join them. Guess dad wasn't ready for that. Neither was mom.

So he took off and joined the service. He turned out to be a war hero, and won a silver star. After he was discharged, he went up north where he had some shirt-tail relatives, cousins, I think, and bought a mobile home—mom says it's a used trailer—and he painted it and fixed it up and took odd jobs near Holder's Crossing—know where that is?

No? It's up by the Canadian border. Dad did electrical work, but when he couldn't find enough customers, he sold dope on the side. Once, I typed his name in my computer's search box with quotation marks around it and found an old newspaper article that said he was wanted on felony warrant for embezzlement.

I saw him a few years ago. We met in town for lunch. He didn't want me out at his place. He looked really bad, like he'd been in a fight. We just don't talk anymore. I guess we just don't have much to say.

So basically, my mom had me spend my high school years at the Elysium Academy, the one in Idaho. Ever hear of them? They're all over. The school is supposed to be so good that it's typically rated in the top 10 college preparatory schools in the nation. There's about a dozen of them spattered around the county. It's a place for families of means to put kids when they don't want them around in their private lives. It's like convenience shopping; you pick one out that you like, that's far away enough, and send your kid away for four years.

Did I *have* to go? You're probably wondering, right? It's like this: they tell you anything to get you there—recreational opportunities, social clubs, students who are the kind of kids you want to be around—anything to get you through the front door. Then you're theirs.

Once you're inside, you can't leave. Don't believe me? Just listen to this: there's a merit system, and if you get so many merit points, you get a pass for a weekend. But no one ever gets a pass. That's the joke: in the history of Elysium Academy no student ever had a weekend pass, and no one has ever heard of anyone who's *had* a pass.

You see, you keep getting demerits—for just about everything—the way you make your bed, what you say to the attendants, your attitude, your grooming, it goes on and on. You're only there a couple of weeks and you have so many demerits, you can never get enough merit points to go anywhere. Besides, there's a first class electrical security system, and they keep all the outside doors locked with a series of checks, so you can't get out.

Then there are 'disincentives.' Ever hear of those? No? I thought not. Students are given a disincentive when they speak in line, or when they're late, and it could be anything, late for morning line up, late for lunch call, late for lights out, late for class or for counseling sessions. For example, scrubbing down the kitchen floor is a disincentive. So is cleaning the toilets in the bathrooms. The biggest disincentive—the one all the kids dread—is being sent to the fan room.

Ms. Tyler-Ramirez, one of my teachers, kept her class together with this one threat alone. I thought I was her favorite. She called on me regularly. And she always said good things about me—how I took care with my appearance, my manners, waiting for others to speak—then she turned on me.

I skipped gym class. Sure, it was a bad idea, but I hated it. I hid out in the rec room. Well, wouldn't you know, it was Ms. Tyler-Ramirez's prep period and she was assigned to walk through the school and check for kids ditching classes. She found me under the pool table.

"I have to report this," she said.

"I know."

"You could be sent to the fan room," she smiled. "Do you want to go to the fan room?"

"No," I said.

"If you do anything like this again, you will become a member of the fan club, I promise. Do you understand?"

I said I did understand, I understood very well, and I never wanted to be a member of the fan club. I heard about other students who were sent there, and when anyone asked them about it, they refused to talk. That's how bad it was.

From then on, Ms. Tyler-Ramirez never gave me another compliment in class, like she did before, and things were tense, but nothing I couldn't live with, and then Mary Donnelly, who sat across from me, wanted me to pass a note to her boyfriend.

I was kind of stuck in the middle, but I gave in—it was only a onetime thing Mary promised—and when Ms. Tyler-Ramirez was adjusting her power point, I took the note and held it out to Mary's boyfriend, but at the same time I was holding the note out, he turned to whisper something to another student. Right then, some students laughed, and when that happened, the teacher turned around and the first thing she saw was me holding out that folded piece of paper.

She came over to my desk. "What do we have here?" she asked, then took the note from me.

She opened it, then handed it back to me. It said:

> Pass this on to Jeff.
> Love, The Class.
> P.S. You've been had.

I don't think Ms. Tyler-Ramirez even read the note, and if she did, she didn't care what it said, not really. The only thing she cared about was sending me to the fan room as a 'disincentive'.

I don't know which was worse: knowing I was going to the fan room, or being set up by the class. Maybe they were jealous because they thought I was teacher's pet, or maybe they just didn't like me and wanted to play a prank.

Anyway, that's how I became a member of the fan club. It works this way: they wait until after you finish lunch, then an attendant announces your name in front of everyone in the dining hall, and then he comes to your table to escort you to the fan room. From that moment on, until the end of time, you're branded. No one wants anything to do with you. You can forget your social life at the school, your friends, even your teachers. They all avoid you.

When you arrive at the door of the fan room, the attendant takes your watch, makes you empty your pockets, purse, and checks to see if there's anything you have that you could use to hurt yourself.

Then you're locked in for the rest of the day and aren't released until after supper.

Yeah, you want to know what you do in there, right? Well, you think, then you get afraid. I tried to remember that everything is a wonderful mystery, you know? And it worked for a while, then sensory deprivation set it. That's something else.

When the door is finally opened, it's dark and the only place to go is to bed. But there's still one more job to do before you can leave.

The room is all white with a linoleum floor. There aren't any windows, and only one air vent. The place is crowded with fans, like a fan forest. They are tall and white. If you walk around in the dark, you bump into them, and you imagine they could start up at any time, but they never do. That doesn't stop you from thinking that they will.

Some family sent them as a gift to the school, to cool things off, I guess, but they were never used. They're just put in storage. I don't know why. I would have plugged on it just to get some air, but there isn't one plug in the fan room.

There is a light bulb socket, and it has a chain dangling from the ceiling. It's empty, and even if you had a light bulb, you couldn't get up that high to put it in. You could yell all day and no one would ever hear you. So all that is left to do is sit it out. I curled up in a corner and tried to sleep, but I couldn't.

When the attendant arrives at night, he has a bucket, paper towels, and cleaning fluid, which is really disinfectant. If you made a mess, you have to clean it up.

After that, nothing was the same. In my junior year, I came up for tutoring assistant, which is an honor, and I was qualified too, but I was passed over because I had been in the fan room.

That's about all I have to say. I know other students want to see you, and I'm just holding them up—

I'm not? Well, let me leave my email address, maybe we could stay in touch. I've really enjoyed your class. I've always admired good teaching.

# NIGHTKEEPER

DAWN. VISITORS NOTE the quality of light here in this part of the country but it's become a cliché. The light is cold and clear they say, when it's more than that. It's the sense of atmosphere itself, heightened somehow as if issued from the surrounding mountains. It's a clarity that suffuses the body. Artists come from all over the world hoping to bring it out in their paintings.

Every morning when I pull back the curtains and look down on the park across the street, the inhabitants come to life as if in a theatre production; the homeless with their carts and bags, runaway dogs, wild by any account, possibly two or three painters out with easels trying to imitate that atmosphere as if once captured, it would be theirs forever.

It does last forever, or so it seems, taking it in from the window of my room. It was in this square I first met Tuli, and only because I was trying to do a good deed, but that kindness turned problematic once I understood his mission, which was not his alone, not at first, but something cooked up by Mars.

Mars—the night attendant at the registration desk—took me aside late one evening and asked if I wouldn't mind taking a sandwich to his friend in the morning, that is, if he showed up.

"He's been away for some time now," Mars said. "Maybe he returned to the mountains, but I am concerned . . ." his voice trailed off and he looked down at his guest ledger. He makes notes on the guests, their preferences and complaints, and only uses the desk computer when he has to, when printing out receipts, and the like.

I don't know what the hotel management would do without him. If someone's working late, say the resident who is a historical researcher down the hall, Mars will take up a pot of coffee, or as in the case of Ms. Dremitus, a widow several times over—must be in her 80s by now—he'll take up a late night snack, maybe a banana from the kitchen after the workers have gone home.

During a mid-day lunch—the hotel provides one meal a day for the third-floor residents only—in the Silver Room, Ms. Dremitus turned to me and said, "I had a difficult night."

"How so?" I asked.

"I couldn't sleep. Not a wink. I was up until 2:30."

"I'm sorry to hear . . ."

"Then I rang for Marston, and he was up in a flash with a tiny white pill. You know how I don't care for medications, but he assured me it would make everything right again, and so it did! I slept soundly until late this morning."

And so it went, Mars scurrying around from one guest's illness, or concern to another, all through the night. He's nearly mercurial, his white pony tail bobbing behind him as he moves about, and his spritely voice despite his age, rapid and a bit high pitched but not irritating as one might expect. Some guests find him irresistible. How many times have I come in late, and asked for a pot of hot water for tea to take to my room, and he produced it immediately? So when he asked me to take the sandwich to Tuli, I agreed. It seemed effortless—I visit the park often—besides what harm could it do?

The owners of the hotel, the same family who established The North American Trust Co. which manages the place, insists the residential floor has suites, not rooms. This is generous of them. So it was from my room, when I pulled back the curtains in the morning, that I would check to see if Tuli was in his usual spot.

Whenever he visits the park, he sits cross-legged atop a pile of boulders off to one corner, arranged by the city for visual effect, a kind of natural decoration. I could see he wasn't there, but I went down anyway, taking my morning newspaper and that sandwich wrapped in butcher paper in my coat pocket in the event he showed up.

I usually find a bench near the street—the city maintains them regularly—one with painted green slats and wrought iron arm rests, and read the news in that light which is cold and so perfectly clear it could etch glass.

When I heard that ancient chanting, I knew Tuli had arrived. There he was, sitting on his rock, looking upward with his eyes half-closed.

Once he paused, I walked over, sandwich in hand.

He looked down at me. "You have something there."

"Yes, something from Mars."

"Mars is my friend."

I held out the sandwich.

"You do not think I can feed myself?"

I placed the sandwich on a ledge of rock.

"No, not at all. But I must ask, why are you chanting?"

"I am singing to The Great Spirit for you to go away," he made a sweep with his arm as if to remove an annoying thing.

"Well, anyway, good to have met you, Tuli," and was about to go on my way when he said, "Tuli is not my name."

"What then?" I asked.

"You cannot say my name."

"Why is that?"

"You cannot say my name."

Then he said his name.

"Now you say."

I tried to reproduce the sounds he made.

"You see, now?"

"I see."

"You call me Tuli for that is how my name sounds to you. It is so for all my people."

He bent down, picked up the sandwich, set it beside him, then pulled on a brass button from what looked like one of those black military overcoats for formal occasions, and when it wouldn't give, he jerked it free.

"Here," he said, giving me the button. "This is not for you. This is for Mars."

THAT EVENING, soon as Mars came on, I went down to the desk and recalled my meeting with Tuli, saying he was grateful for the gift, and surrendered the brass button. Mars pulled a jar out from under the desk, removed the lid, and dropped the button which clinked when it hit a few others, several large unstrung beads, some bird feathers, a pair of unused shoelaces still wrapped in cellophane, and a pocket comb.

"Tuli's people no longer exist," he said, "so he has no family," and explained he was the last descendent of a tribe that pre-existed any of the known pueblos in the San Cristobal Mountains.

"And what is the name of his tribe?" I asked.

"O'Na," Mars said. "The anthropologists that work in the Native American ruins here claim there are eight pueblos. When I asked about Tuli's people, they say it must be 'the ninth pueblo,' which is their way of saying they don't know about it and it's probably a local myth."

"O'Na," I repeated. "And what does O'Na mean?"

"I never learned what it meant," he smiled. "Tuli says I say it wrong, and I wouldn't understand it anyway. It has something to do with being and place, something about what they are to each other, and that's all I know," he shrugged, looking at me with his pale blue eyes, and wearing those slight silver earring loops that glinted whenever he turned his head. I imagined they too, may have been yet another gift—from Tuli, probably for items pilfered from the hotel's kitchen.

At that moment, Ms. Dremitus stepped up to the desk—she had been sitting in a tall-backed chair in the lobby, apparently listening to our conversation.

"Did I hear Mr. Tuli's name mentioned? If you don't mind my saying, he seems lonely. He probably needs a woman. So many men do," she smiled first at Mars who looked down, then at me, her blue eyes twinkling. "Don't you think it's—well—just natural?" When no answer came, she smiled again, and before returning to her armchair in the lobby directly behind us, situated in front of the large plate glass window, she told Mars she hadn't been sleeping well, and could he offer any suggestions, and at this point, Mars reached into the side pocket of his black blazer with HOTEL ST. LYON scrolled with red thread, in a casual cursive across his breast pocket, and produced a tiny glass vial. He shook out several of those little white pills, and when he turned them over to Ms. Dremitus, he said, "These should do you for a while, but please keep in mind, no more than one per night."

ONE OF THE MOUNTAIN storms came in later, after I had gone upstairs and fell fast asleep. Flashes pulsed through my room with the speed of erratic strobe lights. When I pulled the drapes together, it didn't prevent the white bursts from lighting up the place. I turned on a lamp and sat in bed trying to read. Soon as I became absorbed in a passage, another crash would disrupt my attention. When it all quieted down, I thought I'd get some rest, but that wasn't the case. I heard an ambulance siren, and when I pulled back the drapes, there it was in the street below, with its blue and white lights flashing.

Then there was the commotion in the hall; the sound of running, then banging against the wall, as if struck repeatedly by an object.

When I opened my door, I saw several emergency medical technicians hurrying about. They had brought up a gurney to the residents' floor and before I knew it, Mars ran up to me and said, "It's Ms. Dremitus. They're taking her to the hospital," and he was off once again, following the cart down the staircase to the waiting ambulance.

THE MANAGEMENT tried to replace Mars with a temp for the next two nights since he insisted on staying with Ms. Dremitus while she was in the hospital, but it didn't turn out. The guests—especially the residents on the third floor—complained about the stand-in, who could never give them the attention they had received from Mars.

After the third day, I wandered out one afternoon, visited several nearby shops, then decided to go myself to the hospital to find out what was going on.

The old lady was in one of the private rooms, and when I spoke to the floor nurse she told me Ms. Dremitus was resting and shouldn't be disturbed.

"Prognosis?" I asked.

"Anticoagulants, physical therapy, the usual," she replied. "With strokes of this magnitude, it's difficult to say just how long it will take to recover."

"Just how serious is it?" I asked.

"Well," she sighed, "the patient has lost most of her speech, and her right arm, including hand and digits, is paralyzed. So there's lots of work to be done," she smiled the kind of smile that said, "There now. Please, I have work to do."

Before I left, I walked by her room and poked my head in. There she was, lying on her back, her mouth open wide, snoring. And there, seated at the side of her bed, keeping vigil, was Mars himself, asleep in a chair.

Just as soon as Ms. Dremitus was conscious enough to understand what had happened to her, she tried to dress herself; made it known she wanted to leave though everyone—doctors, nurses, even Mars— objected, saying she needed a longer period of time to be properly monitored and cared for.

She'd have none of it. Mars had to make the arrangements to get her back to the hotel as soon as possible.

Once there, she remained in bed, and had little notes made up that she could sign.  On the top of the paper, it read:  FOR:  and this was followed by whatever she wanted—she would somehow communicate this to Mars using a combination of vocal sounds, pointing with her good hand to photos, or making images with paper and pencil, crude though they were, of her needs.  Then he would write them out in longhand, and below each form was this: AUTHORIZED BY:  filled in with an erratic signature she made using her left hand.  In this way, Mars could obtain things for her.  She authorized Mars as a co-signer to her checking account.  All of this put a burden on Mars—Ms. Dremitus's daily needs—his nightly duties—it all caught up with him soon enough.

"I'm not in any condition," he confided one evening after a few days of caring for Ms. Dremitus, "to meet with her sister, you know." Apparently, the hospital had made a note of her nearest relative, a sister who lived in the east and on hearing of her sibling's misfortune, soon as she could put her own things in order, booked a flight into one of the regional airports in the area, then planned to rent a car and drive up into the mountains.

"From what I understand," Mars added.  "Ms. Dremitus and her sister have their differences.  That's putting it gently.  When I announced she planned to visit, I was instructed to dissuade her, something I've been unable to do," he paused and took a breath. "Then on top of it all, is that business with Tuli."

"What business?"

"I promised Ms. Dremitus—and I shouldn't have, but I did nonetheless—I promised her I would try to find a— a— companion for Tuli."

"Is that all?"

"No, but that's all I can discuss at the moment."

"Do you intend to make good on your promise?"

"Yes, I must."

NOT LONG AFTER Mars befriended an elderly jewelry maker who sold her wares from an Indian blanket spread under an archway near the old plaza downtown, he would be released from his promise.

I learned of it this way: I was in a shop doorway late one afternoon, and I could see—reflected in the glass—Mars across the street, bowed over, speaking to the old woman who sat on her blanket with her silver goods set out in front of her.

When I turned around, Mars looked over immediately, abruptly ended his conversation, then walked hurriedly across the street.

"This is what I meant," he said, "when I told you Ms. Dremitus wanted me to find Tuli a companion," and went on to say the jewelry maker—who came from a pueblo not far from Tuli's—had a granddaughter who was encouraged to come into town just to look at Tuli in the square without him ever knowing he was being so regarded. The granddaughter seemed to agree that Tuli might qualify as a prospect, but it was conditional: she wanted to meet with him, naturally, which was the report Mars was getting that afternoon from the grandmother in the square, and of course, there was Tuli's view to consider on the entire matter.

Mars was sweating, probably from all of his hard work, and dabbed his forehead with the turquoise silk scarf he was wearing. He swore he had found Tuli's better half, but there was a provision. "So now, I must speak with Tuli and arrange a meeting. First, I must think out how to break the news to him."

"News?"

"Yes, you see the granddaughter, as attractive as she is, had a child by a man who 'took the long walk.'"

"You mean he's gone?"

"Exactly. The long walk is a journey from which there is no return. What's more he doesn't appear to have any interest in his son—"

"The granddaughter's child?"

"Yes, he hasn't visited the boy for years. He's seven now, and doesn't remember ever having seen his father."

WE BOTH RETURNED to the hotel together. Mars was about to go on his shift, and when he came around to the desk, spotted a note that had been left for him from the day registration clerk. It was a notice from Ms. Dremitus' sister, saying she would be arriving by the end of the week, which was coming up fast, a matter of a couple of days. In addition, she had made reservations at the hotel, expressed her regrets about her sister's illness, and looked forward to seeing her sister once again, and of course, meeting Mars.

He held out the notepaper: "I've messaged her myself. Twice, in fact, telling her that her sister needs bed rest and should avoid excitement, company, and so on; that maybe she might reconsider her intentions, and avoid the visit, certainly at this time."

Clearly, he didn't know what to do, and after a few moments of frustration, changed the subject.

"I've arranged a meeting," he announced. "And I'd like you to join me at the square tomorrow, if at all possible. You see, it is sometimes difficult to persuade a person to do the right thing for himself, and should this occur, you could assist me in helping our Tuli understand his situation, and the opportunity that has knocked on his door, so to speak."

Here he tried to pronounce the name of the jewelry maker, the grandmother, and her granddaughter, and grimaced at his efforts, then said, "The grandmother said I should just call her granddaughter 'Sally.' They will be there as well, at our little meeting."

"Tell me," I said, "does Tuli know about this assembly, or its purpose?"

"No, not at all. I thought it would be best since he might otherwise let his imagination run away with his best interests. We often do this, you know; our expectations somehow pose obstacles."

"You've not spoken with him about Sally then—or her son."

"I've given it some thought, but it might give him a different impression, and I don't want to chance sending him off before he had a chance to actually meet the young woman."


IT TURNED INTO a restless night. I slept in snatches, and dreamed a storm had returned, and the ambulance as well, faintly hearing its wail through the thunder cracks.

When I went down for breakfast, I saw Mars seated on one of the leather sofas facing the fireplace in the lobby. It was embellished with an ornate pattern—columns on either side with angels' wings—and Mars was staring into the empty grate.

As I approached him, he started to get up, and took his coat, the one with the name of the hotel on its breast pocket, rumpled in a pile beside him, and shook it out, then hastily tried to get it on.

I came over and sat down beside him. "No need for that," I said, then took the coat from him, folded it, and set it on the couch.

He looked up at me and shook his head. "I even made flash cards so she could relearn her sounds, maybe regain her speech. It was a vain effort. We've known each other for years. I knew her long before you ever arrived here. Did you know that?"

"No."

"Her name was Martha."

"I didn't know—"

"You didn't hear the ambulance last night?"

"I thought it was a dream."

"I wish it was a dream. Our Ms. Dremitus—my Martha—is gone."

I realized he was inconsolable. My words would have passed over him like water over a rock. He had accompanied her to the hospital for the last time, and sat with her long after the time of death had been determined, and walked back to the hotel and was now staring into that empty fireplace.

"Why not take a few days," I said, "surely you can do that. I can speak to the hotel management, if you like."

"Kind of you," Mars said, "but I have one last duty, as I'd promised her."

"That can't be—"

He looked at me with those bloodshot eyes. "Yes, it can be—."

"Certainly you are no longer bound to any promise you've made. How can you hold yourself responsible now?"

TULI WAS SEATED ON HIS ROCK, chanting. It was barely audible, a low, sonorous series of sounds that were lulling and deliberate, and meditative and slid into their movements as if they emerged from a cave of solace deep in the mountains.

When I came out onto the hotel's porch, I could see that venerable grandmother standing near my bench, across the street, the one I've occupied so often, holding the hand of her granddaughter, who in turn, was holding the hand of her son. The three of them were dressed in their traditional wear for important occasions.

Mars joined me and we walked across the street. He introduced me to the trio, and all of us together approached Tuli, who sensed our coming and ceased his meditation.

"Ah, Mars," he said, "I see you have found a family!"

Sally was amused by this, but not the grandmother. As for the boy, he clenched his mother's hand and looked at her as if trying to understand the scene.

"Hardly," Mars said. "This is not my family—"

"Then whose family is it?" Tuli was quick to interrupt.

"These are my friends, and I thought you might like to meet them."

"Ah. I understand now," he smiled.

Before Mars could make his introductions, Tuli said, "You think I need a woman?"

At this, the grandmother turned abruptly, whispered something to her granddaughter, and stepped back a few paces, staring intently at Tuli.

"You must understand," Mars went on, "Ms. Dremitus commissioned me to try to—" here he broke off, searching for words, "to try to make things better, and I understand this sort of thing might be seen as intrusive, although she, and I have the best intentions—"

"Of course. Intentions."

"And I just thought—I thought that—" then he turned to me as if I had some magical whirlpool of words at my side, as if I could convince Tuli of what a man needs, that he does not know he needs.

I was talking before I realized it, and it surprised me what I said. It was if there was some invisible scroll that decided to roll itself out from my mind to my tongue and I listened to my words as though I'd never heard of them before this moment, and that I never thought at all about what they meant: "If I might add a point or two," I began, "you see, Tuli, Mars has nothing but admiration for you, and when it came to his attention that Sally here," at this point Sally smiled at Tuli, "was walking this way, through the park the other day, and noticed you, she mentioned it to her grandmother, who, I should hasten to add, hails from a pueblo close to those of your people—"

"I see the designs in their dress," Tuli interrupted. "We could be cousins," he added.

"Yes, well, in any case, when Sally had expressed her interest in meeting a most admirable figure, here in this square, a most handsome man, then her grandmother, a friend of Mars, could not help but communicate to him her granddaughter's interest."

We all waited, hoping Tuli would respond to in a way commensurate with my supplication.

"You must be a good friend of Mars," he said. "It takes a good friend to say what you have said."

Was he complimenting me on my lie? Was he sincere? Or was he simply being sarcastic? His face did not favor any explanation.

"Do you think you act because you imagine you will save my people?"

Mars and I seemed to speak simultaneously, "No," we said, then I added, "Not at all."

"Because my people have gone. Now there is only Tuli. And he cannot change nature when nature has made up its mind. I will consider what you say. Give Tuli three days and he will have an answer."

When he looked away, and upward to the sky, it was clear that the conversation was over. The little trio went their way, hand in hand, just as they had come.

On the way back to the hotel, Mars turned to me and said, "I hope Tuli didn't think we were trying to arrange a relationship to avoid the extinction of his culture, or his people, when we were only trying to find him a companion."

"And that's your only ambition," I said.


MARTHA DREMITUS' SISTER arrived on schedule. Before she checked into the hotel, she visited the local funeral parlor where the hospital had sent the remains of her sister.

The director, a tall balding man with a lisp met her in the hallway.

"You must be Ms. Cressida," he said, putting out both his hands to cup hers, "we are so sorry for your loss. I know how difficult a time like this is, and the added burden of planning a memorial service and the extra details have been arranged. So you needn't be concerned."

"Arranged? By whom?"

"Unfortunately, we cannot disclose the names of our clients."

Cressida Dremitus, abruptly withdrew her hands, turned, and left the funeral home, stopping at the first legal firm she could find that specialized in "Estate and Family Law," where she acquired the services of a young lawyer who assured her he would act promptly as her representative, and "get to the bottom of this."

The following evening, the attorney, after making a few calls earlier in the day, was waiting in the lobby of the Hotel St. Lyon for Mars to arrive for his shift.

He handed him his card and said, "I represent Ms. Dremitus, and it is necessary to inventory her possessions, therefore I will need access to her room," and shook out a legal document. "You can see," he said pointing to the bottom line, "it is signed by next of kin, which gives me authority in this case."

"I regret to say the room is unavailable at this time."

"Yes, perhaps, but I am allowed access by law. You see—Mr. Marston, is it?—You see, there is no record of her last wishes, no will or trust, you understand. We cannot assume Ms. Dremitus died intestate. Perhaps her will is still among her papers . . ."

"No," Mars said, "it isn't," and with that, pulled around a necklace, no more than a leather shoelace, until he came to a clump of keys. He held a small one between his fingers. "Is this what you're looking for? It's the key to Ms. Dremitus' safety deposit box, and she had taken the precaution of keeping her important papers in it, including her last wishes—her will."

"I'll take that," he announced, suddenly reaching for the key as if to snatch it from him. Just ask quickly, Mars stepped back.

"I have always followed Ms. Dremitus' wishes. It so happens I was instructed to open that box on her passing. I've done that. And I've inventoried the contents, including her will, in the presence of her own attorney, so there is really no need for you to do anything at all."

ON THE THIRD DAY, we all returned to the park. This time, the grandmother did not come. Sally offered the explanation, "She said she does not think this man would be a good man for me."

"But what does Sally think?" Mars asked.

"Sally thinks Tuli would be a good man."

Then we all went to Tuli's rock to see what Tuli thought.

"Ah," Tuli said, "you have returned."

"Yes," Mars said, "we want to know if you've considered this— this— opportunity—"

"I have done so."

"And what does Tuli think?" Mars asked.

He took a deep breath through his nostrils, and looked away from us. "Tuli does not need a woman."

With this announcement, Sally smiled politely, nodded her head slightly, secured her grip on her son's hand, and left the square never to return.

"Surely," Mars said after they had gone, "she is a capable person, attractive and pleasant. Wouldn't she add to your days?"

"I returned to my home, and spoke with my people, and they did not think this would be wise."

"*What?*" Mars said, nearly shouting. "What? That can't be. Your people are dead. They do not control what you do. It's your decision."

"It is the will of my people. I know what they know."


MARS DIDN'T GIVE UP on his plan for Tuli's well-being, and his commitment to his dear Ms. Dremitus. After a few days, Mars came up with "the one great project" as he put it, what would define his life.

He wanted to meet in the hotel lobby, off in an alcove where the two of us could talk freely, away from his duties, the co-workers, and guests.

We settled into padded leather armchairs. The lighting was dimmed. Mars had asked for tea to be sent over.

He removed a paperback book from his coat. The cover read: A GUIDE TO THE USE OF THE INTERNATIONAL PHONETIC ALPHABET. "This," he patted the cover, "is what I've been reading for the past several days. You see, I haven't given up on Tuli. I am determined, now more than ever, to fulfill my promise to Martha. What could be a better way? Since Tuli refuses to take a wife, to continue the line of his heritage, his culture, I have offered to transcribe the sounds and meanings of his native language using the phonetic alphabet as the basis of translation. This will not simply be a dictionary, but a working, living compendium, complete with idiomatic phrases, tense constructions, and so on, otherwise lost to the world when he is no longer among us."

His eyebrows went up in anticipation. Mars was waiting for my reaction.

"And you've spoken with Tuli about these ambitions?"

"More than that. We had a long discussion, and he understands the need for such work, and has agreed offer any assistance necessary."

The tea arrived on a tray with a side plate of *petit fours*. Mars poured. It was a deep amber color, something said to have originated from the Native Americans in the area. Mars held his cup with both hands, breathing in the aroma from the steam that curled upward.

When he placed the cup back in its saucer he said, "I've wanted to do this for years, and now I'm no longer concerned about financial considerations."

"I see," I said.

We spoke infrequently then, comments about the quality of the tea or the little cakes, but the idea of Mars pursuing his project was disturbing somehow, maybe because it was unlikely that Tuli would have consented, and I was determined to see him regarding this point.

The next day, I watched the square from my window—and Tuli's rock—until midday, then took lunch in the Silver Room. Later, I went out to the porch, found a corner which still permits smoking, and was about to light up a cigar, when I saw Tuli stroll into the park. Whatever Mars thought, I had to hear it from Tuli himself, and walked across the street to join him.

He told me it was true. He had, in fact, agreed to Mars' project—but not for the same reasons.

Tuli looked at me out of the corner of his eye. "I do not do this for my people. I do this for him, for Mars," he said.

"The sounds of my language among my people are shared in the same home," Tuli explained, and for Mars to understand, Tuli had to take him to his ancestral land deep in the San Cristobal Mountains, "a long walk," he said. "Otherwise, he will not understand my language."

"He wants to share your language with the world so it will not be forgotten," I said.

"When he finds the place where we speak with ancestors, he will not care about forgetting. He will not need his book of marks," he said, referring to Mar's guide to phonetic transcription, which, in his enthusiasm, he had shared with Tuli when he first made his proposal.

I hesitated to ask the question, yet I did: "How long do you expect to be gone?"

Tuli shrugged his shoulders. "It is a long walk."

TWO MONTHS PASSED. Winter came. When I woke in the morning and looked out my window, it was frosted, and I could barely see the park, so often covered in snow. The pile of rocks stood solitary and barren.

I never saw Tuli or Mars again. The hotel management hired another night clerk.

On a late afternoon in February—I hadn't ventured out all day—an attendant rang my room to say a package had arrived at the desk.

It was wrapped in brown butcher paper, tied with sugar string. When opened, I found Mars' paperback guide to phonetic transcription, a thick spiral binder which I assumed was for the purpose of keeping translation notes, with all its pages blank. Tucked behind the book cover, was a note from Mars: "I am learning the language of Tuli's people." It was not signed.

The hotel is all but empty this time of year. The tourists have gone away, and many of the shops are closed for lack of trade. The light remains imperial, brisk, both generous and cutting in its clarity.

Michael Gessner has authored 10 books, and has had work featured in *American Literary Review, The French Literary Review, The Journal of The American Medical Association, North American Review, Oxford Magazine, Rue des Beaux-Arts* (Paris,) *The Yale Journal of Humanities in Medicine,* and others. His prose has been called "Structurally ingenious," (Jonathan Galassi, Farrar, Straus & Giroux,) and "A great talent," (Ray Powers, Scott & Field.) A list of other publications, reviews, and readings may be found at: www.michaelgessner.com. He lives in Tucson, Arizona with his wife and their dog "Irish."

Made in the USA
Middletown, DE
23 February 2022

61726084R00118